Really,
Truly,
Everything's
Fine

Really, Truly, Everything's Fine

Linda Leopold Strauss

Marshall Cavendish
New York   London   Singapore

Marshall Cavendish, 99 White Plains Road, Tarrytown, NY 10591
www.marshallcavendish.com

Library of Congress Cataloging-in-Publication Data

Strauss, Linda Leopold.
Really, truly, everything's fine / by Linda Leopold Strauss.— 1st ed.

p. cm.
Summary: Fourteen-year-old Jill forces her family out of denial when her
father pleads guilty to a criminal act that isolates them from their
friends and neighbors.
ISBN 0-7614-5163-3
[1. Family problems—Fiction. 2. Criminals—Fiction. 3.
Fathers—Fiction. 4. Schools—Fiction.] I. Title: Really, truly,
everything is fine. II. Title.

PZ7.S91245Re 2004
[Fic]—dc22
2003017217

The text of this book is set in 11-point Goudy Old Style.
Book design by Anahid Hamparian

Printed in the United States of America
First edition
1   3   5   6   4   2

To Bill, who makes every day of my life a celebration

Prologue

If I'd known ahead of time what was going to happen, I might not have gotten out of bed that day. Not that it would have made any difference—the damage was already done. It was like there'd been some big earthquake a while before and now things were starting to crack and fall, and every day another piece of the roof would come down or a bunch of bricks or a part of a wall till it felt like everything was going to crash around us. Only no one would admit it was happening, and Markie and I couldn't do anything but cover our heads and hide—at least that was what it felt like at first.

I wish I'd learned sooner what I know now, that you can do something to change your life if you don't like the way it's going. I just wish it hadn't taken me so long to figure that out.

chapter

1

"Stop, cut it out, oh, please, won't you stop?" But the shouting went on, the angry voices, the faces blotched with rage. Jill clutched at raised fists, ducked her head against a rain of fury. "Sto-o-o-op!" she yelled again, and her own voice woke her. Pulse pounding, she turned over and breathed in deeply, drinking in the sight of her own room, her windows coated with frost, her posters on the wall. With whom had she been fighting? Although her heart still raced with terror, she couldn't remember now. Then she heard sounds of a real argument coming from the kitchen. She lay rigid on her bed. Her parents hadn't argued like that in months, not since her dad had come back to live with them.

When the quarrel shut down after a few moments, Jill padded down the hall to take a shower, trying to clear her head, to think good thoughts. "Yeah, right," she said to the tropical fish in the tank by her brother Markie's door.

But she had to shake herself out of her funk: This could be a big day. Candidates for eighth-grade offices would be announced this morning, and though Jill wasn't in the super-popular group at school, she had a good chance of being a nominee. She had known for a week what she was going to wear—khaki jeans, a new cranberry shirt, an almost-new ribbed navy sweater. The trick was not to be so dressed up that people would think she'd been expecting a nomination but to look sharp enough so she wouldn't embarrass herself if her name got on the list.

Jill's short, straight blond hair was still wet when she headed to the kitchen for breakfast. She was surprised to find both her parents still at home—usually Mom was on her way to work by now. She prayed that her mother wouldn't notice the wet hair—if she had to wear a hat to school, she'd have hat hair all day. But Mom didn't pay any attention to her. She was too busy being angry at Dad, banging through the kitchen, slamming cabinet doors as she emptied the dishwasher.

"Where's Markie?" Jill asked quickly, looking around the kitchen for her little brother. Having Markie in the room might head off trouble; her parents didn't usually fight in front of him.

"He's still sleeping," Mom said shortly. "I'm going to drive him to school this morning and go to work late."

"Why? Was he feeling bad?"

"No, I just need to talk to his teacher."

Jill nodded. "Hey, Dad," she said, dropping a kiss on her father's cheek before she sat down at the table, breathing in his familiar smell of clean laundry and after-shave. She regarded her parents warily. Dad seemed pretty normal, sitting in his accustomed place at the cluttered kitchen table with his favorite blue coffee mug and his newspaper. His eyes crinkled as he smiled at her, and he looked fresh and crisp in slacks and a neatly pressed plaid flannel shirt.

"Dave?" Mom said.

"For God's sake, Lib, can't we even say good morning first?"

"No, we can't," said Mom in a voice so ominous that Jill looked up at her in surprise. "You need to tell her, Dave. Right now. And if you won't, I will. She's leaving for school in a few minutes. Do you want her to get this information from someone else?"

Jill felt a familiar clutch of fear in her chest. Why couldn't her mother be nicer? She couldn't bear it if Mom made Dad leave again. Not that Jill had ever really understood why her parents had separated, or why they'd gotten back together. They were such an unlikely couple to start with—Dad was good-looking and full of fun, and a lot more easy-going than Mom, who really needed to lighten up. Her eyebrows these days looked as if someone had taken a stitch in the center of each and pulled too tight.

"Dave?" Mom repeated.

"Please, Mom," Jill pleaded. "It's only ten minutes till the bus and it's nominations day and I just want to grab something to eat . . ."

Without a word Mom poured some Cheerios into a cereal bowl and set the bowl down in front of Jill with a spoon and a paper napkin. Dad sighed and passed the carton of milk. Jill exchanged a sympathetic look with her father and picked up her spoon. The fluorescent lights overhead flickered.

3

"What your mom wants me to tell you, Jilly," Dad said calmly, "is that there was a story in the paper this morning. It's not a hundred percent correct, but the gist of it is that I've been helping the FBI with a case they're working on, and I had to appear in court yesterday because of something related to that case."

"The FBI?" Jill wasn't sure she had heard right. "The real FBI? What were you doing working for them?"

Dad worked for GTB Security, arranging for people to put burglar alarms in their houses, but he'd never gotten involved with the government before, let alone the FBI!

"Well, they needed to catch someone," said Dad. "And because of my job, I was in a position to help them—"

"That's not exactly what it says," Mom said dangerously, reaching across Jill to grab the newspaper and slap it down in front of Dad. "Read her the article, Dave. I should have known I couldn't trust you to give it to her straight. Read it. Let her hear what her friends will be hearing. Tell her you could go to jail for this!"

"I don't get it. It says in the paper you're going to jail?" Jill's voice rose in disbelief. "Why? What for?" She stood up, knocking against the table and sending milk sloshing out of her bowl.

Dad set down his coffee cup. "It's a long story, Jill. The short version is that a man I know got some information that let him steal some jewelry from my clients. And he got the information because of me. So—"

"But that was by mistake, right?" Jill looked wildly from her father to her mother. Her mother's face was unreadable.

"Believe me, Jilly, it was a terrible mistake, and I've

been trying to put things right ever since," Dad assured her. "And I'm going to keep on trying to do just that—"

"Jill!" shouted her friend Mary Kate from outside, banging on the kitchen door. "You ready? The bus'll be here in a minute! Time to go!"

Jill didn't know what to do. Dad wouldn't steal anything—why would he? It didn't make sense. And he wouldn't be sitting at the kitchen table drinking coffee if he'd actually been arrested. Mom must have been exaggerating, at least about the jail business. Jill couldn't stand it when her parents got her in the middle of their fights like this. Why couldn't they just give her the straight information?

"Hey, Jill!"

"One minute," yelled Jill. Why didn't Mary Kate come inside the way she usually did? Jill grabbed her pea coat and her scarf from the hook by the door, then ran into the TV room to get her backpack. Returning to the kitchen, she paused a moment. Her mother stood staring out the window over the sink, her back to the room, her angular body looking somehow diminished under her long skirt and bulky coral sweater. "I mean, is this so bad I'm not supposed to go to school, or what?" Jill asked hesitantly. Mom didn't move.

"Mom?"

"Of course you should go, Princess," said Dad, getting up to give her a kiss. "It's a big day. Call me on my cell phone if you get any news."

Mom turned. "Go ahead, Jill," she said. "Keeping you home's not going to accomplish anything. You're better off at school. I just wanted you to know what's going on so you wouldn't be caught by surprise."

"But I *don't* know! What's going to happen? Will anyone be here when I get home? Is Dad going to get a lawyer?"

Mary Kate banged on the door again. "Last call, Jill. I'm freezing. I'm also leaving, so get yourself out here!"

Jill looked at her mother. "Go on," Mom said again. She shooed Jill to the door.

"But—"

"*Now*, Jill. Or you'll be late. I don't want to have to drive you to school, too."

"Okay." Jill turned reluctantly and opened the door. "Bye." A blast of wintry air assaulted her. "Bye, Dad," she called back quickly over her shoulder. She hesitated for a moment, then wound her scarf more securely around her neck and started running through the snow up the driveway. Mary Kate, hurrying up the hill, had left a trail of footprints for her to follow.

"Hey, what's with you, slowpoke?" Mary Kate said when Jill caught up to her. Her nose and cheeks were as scarlet as her puffy down jacket. "Don't you even remember what day this is?" Jill nodded. Mary Kate looked at her. "You're bummed out about that stuff in the paper, right?"

"Oh no, you saw it? Does that mean everyone else at school's going to know, too?"

"My mom and dad were hoping there was some mistake." Mary Kate picked a chunk of ice off a bush by the edge of the drive and examined it. "So was there?" she asked Jill. "Some mistake, I mean?"

"I don't know. My mom was freaking out, but my dad wasn't even acting all that worried. Not that I could get anyone to tell me what's really going on."

"Probably the newspaper was wrong then. I mean, not to be down on your mom or anything, but she does freak out pretty easily." There was a loud hiss of brakes. "Ohmigosh, there's the bus!" Mary Kate started running the last several yards to the bus stop. "So are you psyched about today, Jill?" she asked breathlessly over her shoulder as the yellow school bus groaned to a halt and the driver opened the door. "Can I be your campaign manager if you get something?"

"Sure, I guess," Jill said automatically, but suddenly she felt as cold inside as she did outside, colder than the icicles hanging from the underside of the bus, colder than Mom's voice had been earlier when she was speaking to Dad. Why did the *Times-Register* have to print that stupid article anyway? Climbing on to the overheated bus at Mary Kate's heels, Jill dropped her backpack on the floor. A few eyes met hers, then shifted quickly away. Before anyone could say anything, Jill sank into an empty seat and pulled Mary Kate down next to her for cover. Staring straight ahead, she wrapped her arms tightly around herself and tried to stop shivering as the bus pulled away from the curb.

chapter 2

The minute the yellow school bus stopped in the circle in front of the school, Jill grabbed her things and headed for the door. Cindy Shea was waiting for her at the bottom of the steps, clapping her gloved hands and stamping her feet to try to keep warm.

"Guess what, you're on the list," she told Jill excitedly, her words coming out in small puffs in the cold air. "You did it! I sneaked inside and looked at the bulletin board. You got nominated for treasurer!"

"I knew it, I just knew it!" exclaimed Mary Kate, bounding down the bus steps after Jill. "Who's she running against?" she asked Cindy, squeezing Jill's arm. "Who got president?"

"Ronna Kline and Suzy Kowalski got president, and Maria Juarez and Jonah Karlin got vice president. Just what you'd expect. And Amy Stout got the other treasurer. Jill can beat Amy with her eyes closed."

"With me for campaign manager, she will, won't you?" Mary Kate said to Jill.

Jill nodded happily, hugging the good news to her.

"Hey, guess who's going to be our new treasurer!" Mary Kate yelled to the other kids streaming off the bus. She pointed a finger at Jill and began chanting, "Jill, Jill, Jill." Jill could feel herself blush.

"Hey, guys," said Sheri Leonard, hurrying up the driveway in her furry brown jacket. "How'd you find out already? That's so great, Jill!"

"Cindy did a little spying," Jill told her, grinning with relief.

"Does anyone else know?" asked Sheri.

"No, but they will soon!" said Mary Kate. "I'm going to tell everyone!"

"Tell everyone what?" Robin Liu wandered over from the bench where she'd dumped her basketball gear. "Hey, Jill, that weird story in the paper—was that really your dad? I told my mom it couldn't be."

Jill felt the smile leave her face.

"What story?" asked Cindy.

"Is this about Mr. Rider?" asked Eric Henry. A few more eighth-graders joined the group. "So what's the deal?" Eric asked Jill, his dark eyes sharply curious.

"I don't know. We didn't have much of a chance to talk this morning," Jill said to Eric stiffly. She brushed some hair out of her eyes. She didn't like Eric. With his pointy chin and reddish brown hair, he reminded her of a fox.

"I mean, did they come to arrest him?" Eric demanded. "Like, did you get to see the FBI? Did they come with guns?"

"Jill told me he was home this morning," Mary Kate

told Eric. "How could they have arrested him if he's still at home?"

"People get out on bail," said Eric's friend Russell, pushing his mirrored sunglasses up on his snub nose. "Don't you ever watch television?"

"I can't believe Jill's dad would do anything bad," said Robin. "He's so neat. Isn't he like an American Airlines pilot or something?"

"Oh yeah, I remember!" said Bobby Barrano. "He's that guy who came to school in third grade and turned our class into an airplane."

Jill remembered too. All the parents had been asked to talk about their jobs, and Dad had been taking flying lessons at the time, so for some reason he'd decided to talk about being a pilot. He'd come to school wearing a captain's hat and had thrilled the third-graders by having them arrange their desks like the inside of an airplane and saying they were going to Hawaii. He'd lined them all up and given them boarding passes and then snacks and Cokes on paper trays. For months after, Jill had been the envy of her friends, even though she kept trying to tell them Dad wasn't really a professional pilot.

"That was the coolest project!" said Bobby.

"But the article in the paper said he pleaded guilty," Eric persisted. "Why'd he plead guilty and plea bargain if he didn't do anything?"

"Don't believe everything you read, Eric," said Mary Kate. "Maybe it was a mistake."

"Well, maybe we need to find out," retorted Eric. "I mean, if Jill's going to run for treasurer, maybe we need to know the truth before we trust her with our money."

"You're such a jerk, Eric," said Sheri. "Don't listen to

him, Jill."

"Hey, it's not my dad whose name was all over the paper this morning," said Eric, hauling his book bag up on his shoulder and sauntering toward the front door of the school. Russell, solid as a truck in his burgundy football jacket, followed him into the building.

Sheri looked after them and shook her head. "I bet he's just giving you a hard time because of Amy," she told Jill. "You know, Amy and Russell are like this these days"—Sheri held up a hand with crossed fingers—"and Russell's Eric's best friend. He's just getting on your case so Amy'll win."

"Come on, Jill, let's go inside," said Cindy, grabbing Jill's arm. "I'll show you where the list is. You'll be so pumped when you see your name on it!"

Jill let Cindy usher her into the building and lead her to the bulletin boards, but everything felt unreal, as if she were standing at one edge of the crowded corridors watching herself from a distance. It was as if she were some kind of Jill mannequin, a stand-in for herself. All morning long people came up to her, but half the time she had no idea what they were saying or what she'd said in return—the conversations were all mixed up, sometimes about her father and sometimes about the nomination. Lunch was the most surreal, with some of her classmates whispering about her and others watching her from a distance as her friends chattered brightly across the long cafeteria table, pretending everything was normal.

"Are you all right, Jill?" Mrs. Maylie, her English teacher, asked in her soft, southern-accented voice, coming up behind her as Jill dropped off her lunch tray.

"I'm fine."

"I heard about your dad, and I know it must be hard for you. If you ever want to talk . . ."

Jill nodded, then fled before she betrayed herself with tears. Mrs. Maylie's sympathy frightened her. What did she know that Jill didn't know? Jill also caught other teachers staring at her in class—why didn't they just mind their own business? Jill thought about pleading illness: She needed to be home, to see that Dad's Jeep was still in the driveway, that Markie was okay, that the colors and smells and sounds of her life hadn't changed beyond recognition while she was here at school. But she knew if she pretended to be sick, everyone would get all upset and they'd probably even get the school counselor on her case. Better to wait it out, even if that meant getting back on that stupid bus at the end of the day.

Jill's house and Mary Kate's had a common driveway, so the two girls almost always rode the bus home together and then walked side by side to their houses at the bottom of the cul-de-sac. By the time the bus let them off that afternoon, the sun was fading and the snow in the driveway, which had partly melted during the day, was freezing up again. Jill had to walk along the edge of the drive to keep from turning her ankle on the ice as they started down the hill. Multiple ruts showed there'd been a lot of activity in and out of the house, but Jill saw neither Mom's green car nor Dad's new Jeep in the turnaround. Usually at least one parent was home to meet Markie. Maybe one car was in the garage.

"Let's talk after dinner," said Mary Kate when they got to Jill's front walk. "You call me, or I'll call you, okay?"

"Yeah, sure, see you later," Jill said distractedly as

Mary Kate continued down the drive to her own house. Jill picked her way across the icy path toward the kitchen door. Peeling off her mittens, she retrieved her key from the small red pouch in her backpack. When she opened the door, the house was dark.

"Dad? Mom? Markie?" she called, turning on a light in the kitchen.

"In here, Jilly," called Dad. Jill followed his voice to the living room, where for some reason he was sitting in one of the tall velvet wing chairs usually reserved for company. He had on his leather bomber jacket and looked as if he were ready to go out. Then Jill noticed the two black suitcases on the rug next to his chair.

"Why are the lights off? What're the suitcases for?" she asked, standing in the doorway. "Where's Mom?"

"She went to pick Markie up at school. I was just waiting to tell you good-bye."

Jill's heart began pounding. "What do you mean 'good-bye'? Where are you going?"

"Well, your mom's pretty upset and asked me to move out for a while." Dad held up a gloved hand, as if fending off an argument. "I don't blame her, Jilly, really I don't. But I just want you to know, I'm going to fight as hard as I can to get this thing straightened out. I swear to you I will. Because my goal—my absolute bottom line—is to be here for you and Markie. And I'll do whatever I can to make that happen."

"But where are you going?" Jill's eyes widened. "You're not going to *jail*, are you?"

"No, I'm going to find a rented room or someplace to stay till I can get things squared away." Dad shook his head. "You know, they really never should have charged me, Jilly, after all I did for the FBI. They actually had me wired with a microphone, and I had to get this guy to incriminate himself and record it on tape. I probably shouldn't tell you this, but it was pretty scary. I'm not anxious to do that again."

Jill couldn't believe she was having this conversation with Dad—her own father!—in her own living room. Dad was impeccably dressed and groomed as usual, looking as if he were heading out to a meeting or lunch with his friends, but the words coming from his mouth were bizarre television words, about the FBI and wires and people incriminating themselves. Did he have any idea how strange this was?

The trouble was, Dad kept starting in the middle, and Jill needed a beginning-middle-end story. She also needed to know why Mom would kick Dad out of the house so suddenly. Why couldn't he stay here and "make things right," as he said? Other people got into trouble and their families stuck with them. Dad had said over and over again that he was trying to straighten things out—couldn't Mom give him a chance? Jill didn't want him to leave! Her dad had always been the one who let them act goofy in this house, the parent she and Markie could go to, the one who stuck up for them when Mom tried to run their lives by some stupid rule book. And this was her and Markie's house too, wasn't it? Shouldn't they get to have some say in this?

"Dad," she ventured, "what if we waited to see if Mom changes her mind? She was probably just super-mad for a while. You know how she is. But when she sees how much Markie and I—"

"I don't think so, Jilly. And I really have to leave now.

14

Really, Truly, Everything's Fine

Your mom wanted me to tell you good-bye in person, but I need to be out of here before Markie gets home. He's going to be too upset when he finds out I'm leaving."

Jill stared at him. "You're not going to stay and tell Markie?"

"This isn't so easy for me either, Jill. This is really killing me—I'm not used to being the bad guy around here. I'd do anything for you two kids, you know that."

Well, then, stay! Jill wanted to shout at him. *That's what we want!* But instead she stood stiffly and waited to see what her father would say next.

He rose and picked up his bags with his usual grace, then came over to kiss her gently on the forehead. Tears flooded her eyes. Dad's eyes filled with tears too. "I love you, Jilly," he said softly. "Don't ever forget that. And I'll get this worked out for you. I swear I will."

"But where are you going? What'll I say to Markie?" she pleaded. "What if we need you for something? Where will we find you?"

"As soon as I have an address, I'll let you know," Dad said. "In the meantime, you have my cell phone number." He ruffled her hair. "You didn't call me from school. What happened with the elections?"

Jill sniffed in hard. "I got nominated."

"What office?"

"Treasurer."

"That's my girl. Who's the competition?"

"Amy Stout. You don't know her." Each word Jill spoke felt like a rock dropping into a void. Heavy. Dull. Meaningless.

"Well, I know you, and you'll do fine, Jilly," Dad said. "I'm counting on you. You've always been a winner in my book, you know that."

Jill wanted to fling her arms around him, to grab at his leather jacket, to block his body so he couldn't leave. But he was already moving smoothly toward the kitchen, suitcases in hand.

"Love you, Jilly," he said over his shoulder as she followed him.

"Love you, Dad."

He kissed her again. Wrapping her arms around herself, she watched helplessly as he opened the kitchen door, letting in a blast of frigid air. Then he slung his hang-up bag over his shoulder, turned one last time to look at her, stepped out into the purple January twilight, and was gone.

chapter

3

Still in her pea coat, Jill stood in the middle of the kitchen for a moment, then collapsed into a chair. Her whole body was trembling. She pulled her jacket closer around her and listened numbly as the automatic garage doors opened and shut and Dad's Jeep roared up the driveway. How could he drive so fast on all that ice? Mom would kill him if she ever found out.

The morning *Times-Register* was still sitting on the table, Dad's half-empty coffee mug beside it. Jill's eyes found the headline immediately: LOCAL MAN PLEADS GUILTY IN $6 MILLION JEWEL THEFT RING. She picked up the paper, her hands shaking so badly they made the pages rattle, and read the article.

> David Rider, 39, of New Milford, was arraigned Tuesday in U.S. District Court before Magistrate George Panos for his role in a $6 million jewel theft ring. Under a

plea bargain agreement with federal prosecutors, Rider admitted to one count of interstate transportation of stolen property. Rider, the son of the late Henry Rider, former president of Rider Industries and local philanthropist, was released on a recognizance bond.

Paul Strade, the alleged mastermind of the theft ring, was arrested last month and has been indicted on charges of conspiracy in interstate transportation of stolen property. According to FBI officials, the burglary ring he headed is linked to more than seventy-five break-ins in four states since 1996. Prosecutors say Rider's position as a security systems representative put him in an ideal position to spot valuables in the homes of wealthy area residents. Further arrests are expected.

Under the plea agreement, Rider is cooperating in the investigation and may be called to testify against Strade. In exchange, no further charges will be filed against him. Assistant U.S. Attorney Louis Teixera said Rider's work in taping conversations with Strade was key in helping the FBI break up the jewel theft ring. The specific act for which Rider is being charged is transporting a $150,000 emerald necklace from Lexington, Kentucky, to Chicago, where he turned the necklace over to associates of Strade. Rider faces up to ten years in prison and a $250,000 fine.

chapter

4

"For crying out loud, what do they think it is, a
funeral?" Mom said angrily when she got home a half hour
later with Markie and saw the casseroles on the counter.
Jill had been keeping an anxious eye out for her, but every
time a car had ventured down the driveway, it had turned
out to be someone bringing a container of beef stew or
tuna casserole or bean salad.

"I don't know. They just said they wanted to do something," said Jill. "Or they were thinking of us. Something
like that. I thought it was weird too—I didn't even know
who one lady was, but she left a note. How're you doing,
Markie?" she said, bending down to hug her little brother.

"I'm okay. Is Daddy getting home soon?" asked
Markie.

Jill glanced at her mother. "No, he had to go somewhere for a few days," she said. "But he said to tell you he
loved you."

"Where did he go? When's he coming home?" Markie asked.

Mom was hauling things out of the refrigerator, presumably to make room for the casseroles. Was she going to answer Markie?

Apparently not.

Jill ruffled Markie's silky hair. "I don't know when he'll be back, Markie," she said. "Soon, I hope."

Jill loved her seven-year-old brother more than just about anything. He was so beautiful, with the little hollow at the back of his neck, his shell-shaped ears, the freckles across his nose. Jill swooped down again and enveloped his slight body in an enormous hug. "So how was school today?" she murmured. "Anything interesting happen?"

Markie shook his head against her chest. "The hamster escaped," he said. "And the water fountain broke. I guess that was interesting."

The phone rang.

"Can you get that, Jill?" Mom asked, her head inside the refrigerator.

Jill stood up and answered the phone, talked for a moment, then put her hand over the receiver. "It's Mary Kate," she told Mom. "Her mom's invited us for dinner tonight."

"Tell her some other time."

Jill relayed the message, then shook her head. "Charlotte wants to talk to you herself," she told her mom.

Mom sighed, set a browning head of lettuce down on the counter, and took the phone. Jill noticed the circles under her eyes were unusually dark; her straight hair lay limp on her head.

Jill went to hang up Markie's ski jacket.

"Isn't Daddy coming home to sleep tonight?" Markie asked, following her to the closet.

Jill shook her head.

"Is he on a trip?"

"Something like that," Jill told him.

"Do you think he'll call—?"

"I'm telling you, that Charlotte's like a steamroller when she gets something in her head," Mom said with annoyance, coming into the hall to hang up her own coat. "She said she'd send Keith to get us if we didn't come on our own. I said we'd go, but we're leaving right after dinner."

Jill felt she might actually throw up if someone didn't give her some reliable information about her father. The minute Markie went to his bedroom to work on his comic strip, she began bombarding her mother with questions.

"Believe it or not, if you read that article this morning, you know almost as much as I do," Mom said wearily, putting the last of the containers back in the refrigerator. "I thought I knew what your father was capable of, but I must say, on this one he took me by surprise." She sat down at the kitchen table and pressed the heels of her hands to her temples. "He sure made a mess of it this time, Jilly. And as far as I'm concerned, it's his mess, not ours. He's just going to have to work it out on his own."

"But maybe he's innocent! He told me they shouldn't have charged him, that he was really helping the FBI with a lot of stuff, even dangerous stuff. Don't you think maybe they just made a mistake? Dad wouldn't steal jewels, Mom! I mean, his job is to *keep* people from stealing things."

"His former job," said Mom bitterly.

Jill stared at her, then said, "Well, I think that stinks! I mean, it's like the whole world's ganging up on him before they even give him a chance. If something like this happened to you, how would you like to lose your job and get kicked out of your house all on the same day?"

"Jill, for heaven's sake, this didn't just 'happen' to him! Didn't you read that article in the paper? I know it's hard, but maybe you need to face some facts about your father. He's not quite the paragon of perfection he makes himself out to be."

"Well, it could be he didn't do what everyone says he did. Did you ever think of that?"

Jill was practically screaming now to block out her mother's hateful words. "He wouldn't just go off to jail and leave me and Markie—he said he wouldn't! Maybe it's you who isn't the perfect one, the one who's always right about everything. Maybe he took off because he doesn't want to be around *you* anymore!"

Mom opened her mouth to speak, her face mottled with angry red blotches. But before she could say anything, someone rapped sharply on the glass panel of the kitchen door. Jill looked over and saw Grandma Rider's face peering through. "I'll get it," she told her mother sullenly.

"Jill? Libby?" Grandma Rider came into the kitchen holding a brown bag in her two hands. She stamped snow from her boots on the little mat by the door. Only Grandma Rider still wore those little rubber boots that fit over high-heeled shoes. "Are you two all right? Where's Markie?"

"We're fine, Mother," said Mom calmly. "Markie's in his room. How are *you* doing? I meant to call you, but . . ." Mom gestured weakly.

"I'm fine," said Grandma Rider. "I brought you a pot roast."

Mom started laughing, a harsh, barking laugh that she tried desperately to turn into a cough.

"For the life of me, I don't see what's so funny," Grandma Rider said. "I only wanted to—"

"I'm sorry, Mother Rider," said Mom, taking deep breaths to calm herself. "I know you went to a lot of trouble to make this for us."

"Well, I did, actually," said Grandma Rider. She set the paper-wrapped casserole down on the counter with a reproving thud and loosened the net scarf that was protecting her hair. "I wanted to make sure that you and the children were well-nourished. And now if I can just say hello to my grandson, I'll be leaving . . ."

"Please, Mother Rider," said Mom. "Don't take it the wrong way. I'd ask you to stay and eat, but the Carrolls have asked us over. Though if you want to go with us, I'm sure Charlotte will have enough. Shall I give her a call?"

"No, thank you," said Grandma Rider, her voice quavering slightly. "I don't think I could bear being with my son right now. I might be able to forgive him for what he's done to himself, but I'll never understand how he could do this to the rest of us. And to have to find out about it in the newspaper . . ."

"Dad's not going to the Carrolls'," Jill told her grandmother. "He's moved out."

"I was going to call you tonight and tell you," Mom added quickly. "He's getting a room somewhere. I'm sure he'll be in touch with you."

"Well, I must say, nothing surprises me at this point," said Grandma Rider stiffly. "Will you please tell Markie I'm here, Jill?"

"Markie!" yelled Jill as Mom winced and glared at her. "Grandma Rider's here!"

Markie came running down the hall.

"Hi, Grandma Rider," he said, skidding to a stop on the slippery kitchen floor. "I was just feeding my fish. Do you want to come see them? I have five tetras and two angelfish and a catfish named Cookie. And next weekend Daddy and I are going to go find us a black molly!"

"Are you okay?" Charlotte asked Mom when dinner was finally over. "For the time being at least?" Mary Kate's older brother, Leo, had taken Markie down to the basement playroom, and the grown-ups and Jill and Mary Kate had retreated to the living room. "I mean, what happens next? Do you have enough money?" Charlotte was wearing a black-and-yellow caftan, which she tucked around her legs as she settled herself with a cup of tea on the sofa next to Keith.

"Who knows?" said Mom. "I'm going to try to keep my head above water and put in the hours for that raise. What else can I do?"

Mom had recently switched to a new job at Midtown Hospital, troubleshooting their computer system, and she was already working around the clock. Jill wondered how she thought she could work even more.

"Well, if you need anything—," said Charlotte.

"We'll be fine," Mom told her firmly.

"And Dave?" said Keith, getting up to put another log on the fire. "Does he have a lawyer?"

Mom shrugged. "Lawyers cost money. And he has no job at the moment, and I don't know if law offices take maxed-out credit cards. Maybe one of his buddies can help him, but as far as I'm concerned . . ."

"You're not going to help Dad with a lawyer?" exclaimed Jill.

Mom pressed her hands to her head. "Look, can we change the subject?" she said.

Mary Kate looked at Jill.

"Sure," said Keith. "Just know that Charlotte and I are here for the asking." He glanced over at Jill. "Jill, you won't stand on ceremony, right? You'll give a shout if you need us?"

Jill nodded. This had practically been her second home anyway since she was Markie's age and Markie was just a baby. Dad had been between jobs then and Keith's teaching job had brought him home early in the day, and they'd all had so much fun together. Dad had acted like a big kid, getting down on his hands and knees and playing games with them. When Mom called them to dinner, sometimes Dad would help them hide and then go hide himself till they all felt guilty and went giggling back up to the house. Mom was usually annoyed by then, but Dad could always dance her around the kitchen and get her happy again.

"Jill?" said Mom. "Are you still with us? Time to go. Will you gather up Markie?"

Jill collected her little brother and found his jacket, then slipped into her own. Charlotte stood for a longer time than usual waving good-bye, the open door behind her flooding the dark, icy driveway with light. When she finally shut the door, Jill had to adjust her eyes to the sudden blackness. She didn't know if she could make it even the short distance home. Part of her wanted to fall into bed, but another part longed to be back at the Carrolls', in all that life and warmth and comfort, with the easy hugs, the colorful furnishings, the whimsical folk art in every corner. Dad had loved the fish sculpture on the Carrolls' living-room wall—he'd always teased Keith about the fish sculpture that got away. The Carrolls' house was so different from her own, where sharp words hung in the corners and the only bright things were Markie's pictures on the refrigerator. "Careful on the ice here," murmured Mom beside Jill, but that was all she said the whole way home. Silently the three of them made their way through the night, pushed open the door of their empty house, and went inside. The light was blinking on the answering machine; Mom walked right by it and into the hallway to hang up her coat as Markie ran past Jill to press the button.

Thank goodness Dad had left Markie a message. Maybe Markie would sleep now, though the phone call had left him full of questions. But at least Mom was dealing with him now—Jill had no idea how to answer his questions. She collapsed on her desk chair, too tired to get out of her clothes, to think about clothes for tomorrow. What would tomorrow bring? What was going to happen to them all?

She still had math homework to do, but she had a study hall tomorrow morning. Maybe she'd read now

26

instead, or write in her diary. That was a good one: How on earth was she supposed to sum up this day? She opened her diary and stared at yesterday's entry. *I'm so excited,* she had written before she went to bed. *I'm afraid to jinx myself. I know it shouldn't be such a big deal . . .*

Jill put down her pen. It was all she could do not to drop her head down on her desk and weep buckets for that person in the diary, for how hopeful that girl had been. Could it have been just yesterday that she'd written those words? How could this have happened to her? Would anything ever be normal again? How in the world could she go back to school and deal with this tomorrow and the next day and the next?

Grabbing her pen again, Jill scrawled I HATE EVERY-ONE! across the diary page in letters so black and hard she ripped the paper. She threw the pen across the room and shoved the book across the desk. She felt like hurling her other books too, her pencil mug, her glass paperweight, anything that would crash and shatter and explode. Instead she slumped down in her chair and waited for her body to summon up the energy to stand and get ready for bed.

chapter

5

Monday, January 23

Stupid saying of the day: "Don't worry, dear. It'll all work out for the best."

First of all, what does that <u>mean</u>? (The cafeteria lady said it to me when I went through the line.) Am I supposed to be glad all this happened? And second of all, how does she even know who I am? Sometimes I think everyone in the whole school knows about Dad. It's not so bad when I'm in class, but I hate, hate, hate the cafeteria! I feel like a bug there that everyone's looking at. Or trying not to look at. I just hope there aren't any more articles in the paper.

Do you know what I dreamed the other night? I dreamed Dad had brought me to camp (or maybe it was a school, because it was in a building with stairs), and he dropped my bag on the steps, and all my underwear and Tampax went flying all over for everyone to see. Mary Kate tells me I'm being weird and no one cares that much about what's happening. But every time I see one of the campaign posters she put up for me, I think about what Eric said about not knowing if they should trust me to be treasurer. I actually wish now I hadn't been nominated. (Probably everyone else does too.)

Dad came by on Saturday to pick up Markie and take him to the hardware store and the tropical fish store and out for ice cream. I was at Mary Kate's, and they didn't even come looking for me. If Dad had told me ahead of time he was coming, I could have been home—all I was doing was sitting there with Mary Kate and her stupid soccer friends while they talked about sports. I don't know how Mary Kate can stand it. Christina Petry's the worst—I don't think she said two words the whole time that didn't have "ball" at the end of them. But Mary Kate's pretty much into sports too. That's one thing we don't agree on.

I talked to Dad twice on the phone, and both times he said the same old same old—that he was trying to work things out. Whatever <u>that</u> means. And that he's staying in an apartment downtown. Mom's at her job all the time so I almost never get to talk to her. Not that she's much fun to be with when she's home. But I think she should spend more time with Markie. Someone should. He's really bummed out about Dad being away again.

Like, join the club.

chapter

6

"Jill, do you want to run over to River City mall with Markie and me?" Mom called to Jill from the kitchen late Wednesday afternoon. "I need to get Markie some new gym shoes before his toes go numb."

"Yeah, I guess." Jill had been having trouble concentrating on her homework anyway. "Does it have to be River City?" she asked her mother, going into the kitchen. "Could we go to Westgate instead?"

"Why in the world would we want to go to Westgate?" exclaimed Mom, who was busy sorting through some files in her briefcase. "It's twice as far, and I just dealt with all that traffic getting home. Anyway, I thought you liked River City better. Isn't that where you and Mary Kate went a couple of Saturdays ago?"

Jill sighed. "Yeah, I just don't feel like running into anyone I know right now."

Her mother frowned. "Is this about what I think it's

about, Jill? Because we can't hide our heads in the sand forever. People are just going to have to get used to seeing us live our lives like everyone else."

"I don't care, I hate it! Mary Kate and I heard two women talking about Dad in the drugstore yesterday, like how he's not living with us anymore, and what's his poor family going to do, and stuff like that. And the way they were saying it was like it was some big, horrible secret, like we were contaminated or something."

"Well, you know what, Jilly? That's their problem. I don't enjoy it when people gossip either, but I'm not going to drive half an hour out of my way to avoid them."

Jill wondered why she'd bothered to say anything. Mom always had an answer for everything—she was always so sure she was right!

"Besides, it's none of anyone else's affair, Jill." Mom stuffed the files back in her briefcase and snapped it shut. "And that's exactly what I want you to say if they ask you."

"Forget I mentioned it," Jill told her, heading toward the door. "I'm not really in the mood for the mall anyway. You and Markie will do fine without me."

"Come back, Jill," Mom said wearily. "If you feel so strongly, I guess we can go to Westgate. Go tell Markie to get his jacket on. I'll meet you back here in five minutes."

The drive to Westgate wasn't as bad as Mom had expected, and once at the mall, Markie found some gym shoes he liked right away. He insisted on wearing them and strutted proudly down the corridor toward the food court, where Mom had decided they could have supper. Jill found a table near the back wall and then went to get food for the three of them.

"Can I go to the pet store to look at the puppies?" Markie begged when he'd eaten his burger and licked all the ketchup from his fingers.

"Just stay outside where we can see you," Mom told him. She settled back in her chair as Markie ran eagerly through the food court toward the pet store. "This was a good idea," she told Jill, pushing her salad away. "I think we all needed the break."

Jill nodded, watching her brother talk to the puppies in the window. "Please, can't Dad come back, Mom?" she said. "It's awful having him living downtown, and Markie misses him even worse than I do."

Mom shook her head.

"Why can't he? Because of you or because of him?"

Mom's mouth tightened. "Because of circumstances," she said.

"What does that mean?" Jill demanded. She balled up her trash and jammed it into her drink cup. "Like, what am I supposed to say to Markie when he asks when Dad's coming home?"

"For now just say he's away," said Mom. "And we don't know for how long."

"That's what I do say, and it drives him nuts! He asks about Dad every ten minutes!"

"Well, it's all I can think of to tell him right now," snapped Mom. "Okay?"

Jill took a deep breath. "Mom?" she said. "Those ladies in the drugstore? They said Grandpa Rider didn't leave Dad any money because he thought Dad needed to learn the value of a day's work. Is that true? Did Grandpa really not give him any money?"

Really, Truly, Everything's Fine

Mom was silent for a moment. "Not a cent," she said finally. "But it certainly isn't anyone else's business."

"But that still doesn't mean Dad would *steal*, does it?" Jill was finding this all very confusing.

"That's a question you'll have to ask your father, Jill. At this point I'm not even prepared to guess what that man would do."

Mom rose from the table abruptly and began gathering up the coats, making it clear their conversation was over. Jill glared at her mother—how was she supposed to understand what was happening if no one would talk to her? And how did Mom expect her to ask Dad questions if she wouldn't let him come home!

Markie wanted to stretch out on the back seat of the car on the way home and look upside down out the window, so Jill sat up front with Mom. She pressed as close as possible to the door, staring at the road ahead.

"Can we tell knock, knock jokes?" Markie asked.

Mom didn't say anything.

Jill shot a dirty look at Mom. Why was she taking this out on Markie?

"Sure, Markie, " Jill told her brother. "You start and I'll answer."

"Okay. Knock, knock," said Markie.

"Who's there?"

"Tank."

"Tank who?"

Markie giggled. "You're welcome. Knock, knock again."

"Who's there?"

"Orange."

"Orange who?"

"Orange you glad I'm your brother?"

"Oh, boy, am I glad," said Jill, turning to look at him. "What would I do without you?"

"Knock, knock."

"Who's there?"

"Robin."

"Robin who?"

"Robin banks isn't a nice thing to do."

Jill could almost feel her heart stop. "Who told you that one?" she asked Markie.

Markie shrugged. "Some boy at school. He made it up. Your turn, Jill."

"Okay. Um . . . knock, knock. . . ."

"Who's there?"

Still off balance from Markie's robin joke, Jill was at a loss.

"If you can't think of one, I'll help you," offered Markie. "Knock, knock, Jill."

Jill swallowed hard over the lump in her throat.

"Knock, knock, Jill!"

"Who's there, Markie?" Mom answered for her unexpectedly.

"Olive."

"Olive who?"

"Olive you and Jill and Daddy," Markie told Mom. "Knock, knock. . . ."

chapter

7

At school the worst part of every day for Jill was lunchtime. She was usually too stressed to eat anyway, so she started hiding in the band room instead of going to the cafeteria. Mr. Moskowitz, the band teacher, always left the room open, and Jill could sit behind the drums and read a book to try and block out everything bothering her. Mary Kate warned her that avoiding the cafeteria was no way to win an election, but Jill pointed out that Cindy was the only one besides Mary Kate who'd even said anything about her being gone. Mary Kate had sputtered, and her cheeks had gotten all red with frustration, but then she'd just told Jill it was hopeless to argue with her and walked away.

Good. Jill didn't want to be with her so-called friends anyway, who had no idea what her life was like right now and didn't seem to care. She'd rather be in here by herself. She took her peanut butter sandwich out of its plastic bag, ate a few small bites, then got up to throw the rest of it in the metal wastebasket next to Mr. Moskowitz's cluttered desk.

"Whoa," said a gravelly voice from the doorway. "I didn't know anyone else ate in here."

Jill turned to see Vanessa Waters filling up the doorway. Vanessa was relatively new at school, and Jill hadn't talked to her much, but they had a few classes together, and everyone knew who Vanessa was—she was too large to miss and too inclined to speak her mind for anyone to ignore her. She was definitely a presence. She made her way through the school halls as if she owned them, usually wearing a long, full skirt and a flowing shirt topped with a huge fringed shawl.

"I was just leaving," Jill said quickly.

"No you weren't. You're leaving because I came," said Vanessa. "But you don't have to."

Jill wasn't quite sure what to say. Vanessa's dark eyes challenged her, as if daring her to come up with a plausible response.

"What are you doing hiding in here anyway?" Vanessa asked her.

Jill felt her temper rise. Who did Vanessa think she was, accusing her of hiding? "What are *you?*" Jill returned.

"That's easy—I hate lunchrooms. I'm really bad at lunchrooms. I mean, look at me." Vanessa held out her arms, the fringe on her shawl swaying with the motion. "I'm not exactly the kind of person girls like you want to be friends with. And people who don't have friends hate lunchrooms. It's as simple as that."

Jill wasn't sure whether Vanessa's frankness was offensive or refreshing. And what did she mean, girls like Jill?

"So that's why I'm here. Now it's your turn to answer. You've got plenty of people to eat with. You're going to be our next class treasurer, for heaven's sake."

The way she said "class treasurer" didn't sound like a compliment.

"Maybe I don't *feel* like eating," Jill snapped back at Vanessa. "And if you really want to know the truth, the reason I'm here is that my dad got in trouble and split on my mom, and everything in my life is a holy mess! So excuse me if I don't want to hang out in the lunchroom today."

Now why had she said that? Jill turned to grab her things. She wasn't going to speak one more word to Vanessa if she could help it. Vanessa was just trying to bait her to see what kind of reaction she'd get.

"Whoa, girl," said Vanessa. "I wasn't trying to give you a hard time. You can eat lunch anywhere you want, as far as I'm concerned."

Jill's eyes swam with tears. She gritted her teeth hard.

"Look," said Vanessa. "Do you want me to go? I mean, you were here first. Or maybe I could stay, and we just won't say anything to each other. We'll make a pact. You can hide behind the drums, and I'll hide behind the music stands. And the first one who tries to make conversation gets banished."

Jill almost giggled. As if Vanessa could actually hide herself behind the music stands! But the truth was, Jill didn't want to be here with anyone, even someone who promised not to talk to her.

"Is that true about your father?" asked Vanessa. "That he got in trouble?"

Jill nodded. "You didn't know about it?"

"Nah, I'm not exactly in the gossip circle. What kind of trouble?"

"I thought everyone knew. They say he was part of a jewel theft ring. He might have to go to jail."

"I guess I'm not everyone then," Vanessa retorted. She held up her lunch bag. "So do I go or stay? I'm kind of hungry."

"I don't care. You have as much right to be here as I do. I'm not even in the band."

"Me either." Vanessa sat down on one of the metal band chairs, reached into her lunch bag, and pulled out a sandwich. "And hey, if I stay, you can practice your campaign speech on me and tell me why you want to be treasurer. It's a golden opportunity. Maybe I'll even vote for you."

Vanessa unwrapped her sandwich; it smelled like bologna. She opened a bag of chips and offered some to Jill. Jill took a couple to be polite, then sat down to eat them, unwilling to give Vanessa the satisfaction of chasing her away. "Girls like her"—what kind of person did Vanessa think she was? She wasn't a snob, if that was what Vanessa meant.

"You really didn't know about my father?" she said to Vanessa. "There was an article in the paper and everything."

"Vanesssa swallowed. "I think I might have read it. But I didn't know it was your dad. I mean, there are lots of people with your name, aren't there?"

"Well, they got some things wrong. At least I think they did. Nobody in my family is really big on explaining things."

"Don't you hate it when that happens? I mean, when everyone shuts down so you're totally clueless? I've sure been there," said Vanessa. She put down her sandwich.

38

"Yeah, but my mom's shutting down on everyone," Jill told her. "I was in the kitchen this morning when some lady called, and my mom said, 'Oh, we're all doing fine, just fine.'" Jill's face twisted a bit as she imitated her mother's falsely cheerful voice.

"Is she always like that?"

"I don't know. I guess mostly she's stressed. She's never been a lot of fun though. My dad was always the one we hung out with."

"So is your dad actually in jail now?"

"No, he's in an apartment downtown. So I'm hoping maybe they're dropping those charges—maybe they've even decided he's innocent. I mean, they'd put a real jewel thief in jail pretty fast, wouldn't they?"

"You'd think."

Jill felt relieved to be talking to someone about her dad. But then a wave of panic washed over her. What if Vanessa was a blabbermouth and everything Jill had just told her wound up as public property? Jill quickly reviewed the conversation, her heart pounding wildly. Had she given away anything really private? Could she count on Vanessa to keep a secret?

She looked across at Vanessa—what kind of person was she anyway? She seemed to be making some kind of statement with her clothes and that tangle of wiry black hair, but Jill wasn't sure what it was. How could she even get a comb through that hair?

"Don't tell anyone I talked to you, okay?" she said to Vanessa hesitantly. "Could we just keep this conversation to ourselves?"

An odd look crossed Vanessa's face.

"Sure," she said, packing up her lunch bag. "Not that

many people talk to me anyway."

"I didn't mean . . . hey, I mean . . . do you want to meet here again tomorrow?"

"Maybe." Vanessa's voice was stiff. "I'll have to see. I've been getting a lot of lunch detentions lately. I don't exactly always get my homework in on time."

"Well, if you can."

What was Vanessa's problem? Did she expect Jill to beg or something?

The bell was about to ring. Jill stood up to get her backpack from behind the drums, then turned to go.

"So maybe I'll see you tomorrow." Vanessa's voice trailed after her.

Jill shrugged.

"Hang in there, little Ms. Treasurer," Vanessa said as Jill headed out the door.

chapter

8

Jill was oddly disappointed when Vanessa didn't show up the next day, or the day after that. Not that Vanessa had made any promises, she told herself; and besides, hadn't she really escaped the cafeteria because she wanted to be alone? Still, Jill couldn't help being miffed—she'd tried to be friendly, and it wasn't as if Vanessa had so many friends to choose from. But then suddenly on Friday there Vanessa was again, seated in the middle of the band room. She was wrapped in a yellow-plaid shawl, her silky emerald green skirt spread all around her, placidly eating a tuna sandwich as if she were queen of the trombones. Jill could smell the tuna all the way across the room.

"So," she said as Jill walked in.

"So what?" Jill said shortly.

Vanessa shrugged. "So have a seat. I assume you're here to eat?"

Jill just stood there.

"Have it your way." Vanessa took another bite of her drippy sandwich, then put it down and unwrapped a Ho-Ho. "Anyway, I was going to tell you—you need some big-time help with your campaign posters. They're really lame. Not that Amy's are any better."

"Mary Kate and I are working on a slogan, but nothing good rhymes with 'Jill,'" said Jill defensively, pushing her hair back behind her ears. "'No frills, vote for Jill.' 'If you don't vote for Jill, you're over the hill.' You wouldn't believe how many bad rhymes we've been through."

"'Vote for Jill to fill your till?'" said Vanessa. She put up her hands before Jill could say anything. "Okay, okay. Did you try 'Rider?'"

"Nothing rhymes with 'Rider' either. But we might do something with a dollar sign for the s in treasurer. Something that fits on a book cover. Mary Kate wanted us to get buttons made, but my mom said it was too expensive. And I need to come up with a fund-raiser for the class. Usually we sell stuff, like that candy people try to get you to buy outside of Shop-Mart. Or nuts. Or stationery. But I want something different."

Why was she babbling like this? Vanessa couldn't be all that interested. In fact, Vanessa had made it clear the other day that she thought the whole idea of running for school office was stupid.

"Stationery," said Vanessa. "Now that's an idea that's going nowhere."

Stationary. Going nowhere. Jill groaned.

Vanessa's lips twitched, and Jill felt as if she'd passed some kind of test.

"So nuts to stationery," said Vanessa.

Oh, my. Raising an eyebrow at Vanessa, Jill pulled up a chair and took out her sandwich.

"How about a totally different project?" Vanessa said. "Like, I saw this neat show in New York a couple of years ago where people made sculptures out of canned goods. And then afterward they donated the cans to a food bank. Some of the sculpture stuff was pretty big—you'd need a humongous room to show it in—but you could get everyone in the class to make things and then charge the parents to get in to see them." Vanessa shrugged. "Anyway, it's a thought," she said before Jill could respond. "So what's this Amy you're running against got going for her?"

Jill blinked. Did Vanessa always jump from subject to subject this way?

"Mostly her boyfriend," she told Vanessa. "Mary Kate's worried that since Russell's a football player, all the jocks are going to vote for her."

"That's *it*?"

Jill giggled, opening a can of apple juice. "Amy's not so bad. Though I think the fact that she's going out with Russell is actually a reason to vote *against* her."

"Russell the Muscle? The guy who sits next to me in Art? The one who thinks a circle is shaped like a football?"

Jill grinned. "That's the one."

"Maybe we should let him make Amy's posters. That'll sure take care of the election."

"You want to know a secret, Vanessa? I'm not sure I even care that much any more." Saying the words, Jill suddenly realized they were true. There was too much else happening in her life—the election didn't seem as important as it once had. "I actually think Mary Kate wants to win this election more than I do."

"Well, tell Ms. Mary Kate you've got my vote," said Vanessa. "But I can't bring a whole team of jocks along with me. Though some people think I'm a team all by myself." She got up, her green skirt swirling around her. "Just more to love is one way of looking at it," she said, walking grandly over to the wastebasket to dust Ho-Ho crumbs off her hands.

"You almost finished?" she asked Jill. "I need to get to my locker before Art. Thank the Lord for Mrs. Eisenstadt; she's the only bright spot in my day. Excuse me—except for you," she said, bowing slightly toward Jill. "See you in Mrs. Eisenstadt's room?"

Jill nodded, wondering why Vanessa always left her feeling off balance. But at least Vanessa didn't tiptoe around her as if she were some kind of charity case, the way everyone else did these days.

"Catch you in Art then," Vanessa said, adjusting her shawl and heading for the door. "Don't be late now. The Russell man and I will be waiting," she called back over her yellow-plaid shoulder.

"What in the world is she doing?" Tiyesha Collins asked Louise Andrews in art class, pointing to Vanessa at the table in front of them.

Jill glanced up from her collage to see what they were talking about. Vanessa was crumpling up pieces of paper and stuffing them into Russell Beck's back-pack. She handled the paper very quietly, so it didn't

44

rattle as she crunched it up. Was Vanessa doing it to be funny? She didn't look around to see if anyone else was watching; she just went about her task methodically, as if it were a usual thing to do. Russell was busy thumb-wrestling with Amy and didn't notice a thing.

"Weird," said Louise.

"Wait till Russell finds out," said Tiyesha.

Vanessa appeared to have run out of paper. She rummaged around in the big black satchel she always carried and took out a bag of cookies. Breaking up the cookies with her fingers, she added the crumbs to the paper in Russell's backpack.

Jill looked up and down her table. A half dozen people on both sides of her had stopped working and were watching Vanessa, mesmerized. Finally Jimmy Choi grinned and called Russell's name, and Russell turned around.

"Hey, what're you doing? Cut that out!" he roared at Vanessa, his face turning bright red. "Mrs. Eisenstadt, make her stop that!"

"I was just trying out some performance art," Vanessa told Mrs. Eisenstadt innocently. "It's called 'That's What Makes the Cookie Crumble.'"

"I'll crumble you!" Russell said to Vanessa angrily.

"We could do without the threats," Mrs. Eisenstadt told him evenly. "And if you're into performance art, Vanessa, let's go on to 'Removing Things from Russell's Bag.' I hope you're prepared to use crumpled papers in your collage? We don't have paper to throw away around here."

"No way is she getting anything out of my back-pack!" said Russell. "I don't want her touching it."

45

"It was clean paper," Vanessa told him. "And they were perfectly good cookies. Oatmeal raisin. I made them myself."

"Vanessa!" warned Mrs. Eisenstadt.

"Sorry, Mrs. E.," said Vanessa. "I just needed inspiration. Maybe crumpled papers will do the trick. It'll give the collage texture."

Mrs. Eisenstadt sighed.

"I think I'd like to see a little less performance and a little more art around here," she said. "Everyone back to work, please. Amy and Russell, you need both hands to do a collage. Do I have to separate the two of you?"

"Russell and Amy *are* a collage," murmured Vanessa. "A work of art," she added quickly as Mrs. Eisenstadt sent her a warning glance. Four or five other students started giggling.

"Did I say 'back to work?'" said Mrs. Eisenstadt, setting Russell's backpack up on the table. Russell turned angrily from Amy and grabbed papers out of the backpack, which Vanessa cheerfully began heaping into a large pile. Jill watched her for a moment, bemused, then reapplied glue to some thin strips of silver paper she was arranging into a grid pattern on her own collage. As she carefully placed the silver strips, Vanessa turned and winked at her. What was Vanessa up to? Jill smiled weakly back at her, realizing she could probably know Vanessa for a million years and not understand her at all.

"I heard what happened in your art class today. Russell's been telling everyone about it," Mary Kate said to Jill at the end of the day as the two of them waited for their bus in front of the school. Jill looked at her watch. Usually the buses were here by now.

"Russell needs to chill. It wasn't that big a deal," she told Mary Kate. "It was pretty funny though. I think Mrs. Eisenstadt actually gets a kick out of Vanessa."

"You two aren't still hanging out in the band room, are you? People think it's weird that you don't come to the cafeteria anymore."

"I don't like the cafeteria," Jill said flatly, dropping her backpack to the ice-covered pavement and winding her scarf a few more times around her neck. She couldn't believe how cold it was! "You don't know what it feels like, Mary Kate. Everyone looks at me funny. Like, do you see anyone coming up to talk to us right now? And not one single person has called me or asked me to hang out since this all happened." Unexpected tears threatened Jill, and she blinked them back furiously. "Crybaby Jill for Treasurer"—now that would make a memorable slogan!

"What about me? I call you," Mary Kate protested. She stamped her feet and wrapped her arms around herself. "Really, Jill, I don't think most people are thinking about it that much. Sheri says you always disappear when she wants to talk to you. If you're running for office, you've got to let people see you."

Across the street, Sheri and Graciela Moreno caught sight of them and waved. Mary Kate waved back furiously.

"Wave, Jill!"

"What, they won't vote for me unless I wave to

them? At least Vanessa'll vote for me. She told me to tell you."

"I don't know how to say this, Jill," Mary Kate said seriously, "but I think you need to be careful around Vanessa. I've heard some pretty strange things about her."

"Like what?"

Mary Kate shrugged. "That she's a bad influence. That there's some big secret in her past. My soccer friends say she carries tarot cards around with her in her backpack. Who knows, she might even be doing drugs."

"Oh, come on, Mary Kate, she's not doing drugs. She's a little weird, that's all."

"Well, people are going to think you're weird if you hang out with her," Mary Kate insisted. "And weird people don't get elected to class office. Besides, now she's got Russell mad at her. You don't want him going around bad-mouthing you. He knows too many people."

"What's he going to do, spread stories that my father might go to jail?"

Mary Kate fell silent, her dark eyes hurt. Jill immediately felt bad. Mary Kate was too easy to tease. She was such a good person, and she really did have Jill's interests at heart.

"Sorry, M.K.," she murmured as the buses started pulling into the driveway. "This is all just getting to me, okay? I'll wave; I'll be a great little candidate. I even have an idea for a fund-raiser."

"Hallelujah," said Mary Kate, who'd been bugging Jill all week to come up with a plan for making money.

Really, Truly, Everything's Fine

"Actually, it's Vanessa's idea," Jill said as the two of them shouldered their way into the bus line. A look of alarm crossed Mary Kate's face. "And it's not selling drugs, I swear, Mary Kate. It's a totally legal plan. You'll love it, I promise."

chapter 9

"Jill, hurry, Dad's here!" Markie yelled late Sunday morning. "He brought me some markers and a fish book. And he brought us all doughnuts. He said we can have doughnuts for lunch!"

Jill put down the English notes she'd been studying and stood up slowly. Now that Dad was finally here, she didn't know how she felt—she was anxious to see him but angry and nervous at the same time. What was she going to say to him? How long was he going to stay? How weird was it going to be to have him back in the house again?

"Hey, sweetheart," Dad said when Jill came into the kitchen. His face lit up in a smile as he walked across the room to hug her. "How're you doing? You up for a doughnut?"

"I don't know. Where's Mom?" Jill said, looking around for her mother.

"She went to work for a while," Markie said excited-ly. "But Daddy bought you a present too, and it's not even anyone's birthday! Daddy, give Jill her box. Don't you want to open it, Jill?"

Dad handed Jill a foil-wrapped box. She unwrapped it carefully, with Markie peering over her arm. Inside was a soft green-and-yellow striped scarf and matching mittens.

"Thanks, Dad. They're great," Jill said, lifting out the scarf. "But you didn't have to get me a present."

"There's more. Lift up the mittens."

Under the mittens was a pair of gold, crescent-shaped earrings.

"Do you like them? Hurry up, try them on," Dad said. "I want to see how they look on you."

Jill took off her old earrings and tried on the new ones. "What do you think?" she asked Dad.

"I think they're beautiful," Markie said.

"I think you're right," agreed Dad. "And your sister's beautiful too. How's the election coming along, Jilly?"

Jill shrugged. "Not much is happening yet, but we've made a few posters and stuff."

"Can we have doughnuts now?" Markie asked Dad, dancing around his father. Jill envied her little brother's ability to pick up with Dad where they'd left off.

"Okay, party time." Dad, set the box of doughnuts in the middle of the table. "Let's have some milk with these so we can get a decent food group into our lunch. Otherwise your mom'll fire me for good."

"No, she won't, Daddy," Markie protested. "She likes doughnuts too."

"I know she does," said Dad, ruffling Markie's hair. "And I bought her her favorites, so don't you eat the cinnamons. I bought jellies for you."

"Jellies are *my* favorites," said Markie happily.

Markie ate three of the jelly doughnuts Dad brought and then complained that he felt sick to his stomach. At least he didn't throw up. Dad told him to lie down, but Markie refused to leave, hanging on his father, clinging to his arm, leaning against the side of his chair. Jill realized quickly that she wasn't going to get a chance to ask Dad about anything Markie wasn't supposed to know. Maybe one day she and Dad could go somewhere, just the two of them. Maybe he could take her to see his apartment. On the phone he'd told her it was pretty simple, just an old couch and a bed and a table. But he must also have had a good shower and an ironing board, because he looked as fresh and well pressed as always. He smelled good, too. Too bad Mom hadn't stuck around to be impressed.

Markie and Dad set to work cleaning Markie's aquarium, catching the fish in little nets and putting them in a small holding tank, dismantling the pump and scrubbing down the glass, and doing other fish things in which Jill had not the least bit of interest. Markie chattered happily to Dad the entire time, making plans for new fish to buy and new arrangements for the rocks and coral. Occasionally Dad would ask Jill a question such as "How's my pal Mary Kate doing?" or "Do you still like your English teacher so much?" but it felt more like polite conversation than real talking.

Finally Dad and Markie got the fish tank back together, although Dad thought they should keep the fish in the holding tank a little longer while the new water in the aquarium settled down. "You can dip them up and put them back later this afternoon," he told Markie. "Just do it carefully—you remember how."

"Where will you be?" Markie asked him.

"I have to leave again. Remember I told you I have to take care of some things?"

"But I thought you'd already done that!" Markie's voice was rising. "Why can't you stay home and take care of them here?"

"I just can't, Markie. I need to be somewhere."

"But I need you here! I don't want you to go!"

"I'm sorry, Markie. . . ."

"It's not fair!" Tears began streaming down Markie's cheeks. He threw down his fish net. "I wanted to show you stuff, and you said you'd help me make a snowman. And I can't do the fish by myself—I'll probably make them all *die*!" Sobbing, he ran into his room and threw himself on his bed.

Jill tore after Dad, who was already on his way to the kitchen.

"He's just a little kid. You can't keep *doing* that to him!" she told him furiously.

"I know he's upset, but he'll calm down in a few minutes," Dad said. "And I really do have to meet someone, Jilly. Will you go see to him for me? I'm sure Markie can move the fish by himself once you calm him down."

"Go see to him yourself! It just makes it worse if you sneak out on him!"

"If I thought staying another half hour would make a difference, I would. But the same thing's going to happen no matter when I go."

Yeah, right, thought Jill bitterly. *And you've got all those things to take care of.*

"I'll be back as soon as I can," Dad said, reaching out

an arm to give her a hug. Then he grabbed an armload of clothes and the bag of CDs and computer disks he'd retrieved from his study. "Your mom should be back any second. Tell her I said not to scold you about the dough-nuts."

Jill could hear Markie still crying in his room.

"Bye, sweetheart," said Dad. "I'll talk to you soon. Could you get the door for me? Give your brother a kiss . . . you're great, I love you!"

Silently Jill let her father out, then slammed the door behind him as hard as she could. As Markie's wails grew louder, she turned quickly, drew a deep breath, and hur-ried down the hall to her brother.

chapter

10

Sunday night, January 29

What a day. I'm so tired. It's weird—we waited all
week for Dad to show up, and then when he came, it just
seemed to make things worse. Markie was crying so hard
when Dad left this afternoon that I was worried he was
going to get sick. So I had to think of something fast, and
then I saw a notice about the hobby show on his floor, and I
asked Markie if he was going to be in it. But he said he didn't
have a hobby. So we started thinking about what might be
his hobbies, and finally I had the idea that the Dino-man
comic strips he's always drawing are kind of like a hobby. So
I'm going to help him put together a display of his best Dino
strips. He's saved a lot of them, so that should work out
really well. ("Hobby" is a weird word—did you ever notice?
It doesn't sound or look anything like what it means.)
Anyway, Markie seemed pretty okay with using his Dinos,
and at least it got his mind off Dad for a while. This family

could actually use a superhero like Dino-man right now.

P.S. Mom pitched all the doughnuts Dad left, but she let us eat frozen pizzas for dinner, and she even had some herself. I can just see the headline: Father Gets in Trouble with Law; Mom Converts to Junk Food.

P.P.S. I was so-o-o relieved that Mom offered to help Markie get the fish back in the tank. I can't stand fish when they're not in the water. I told Markie he should trade them in for hamsters, but he says he loves them too much. How can somebody love a fish????

Wednesday, February 1

This house is getting really nutty. I mean, I'm so sick of it, sick of it, sick of it. Mom's practically never here, and I have to come right home from school every afternoon to take care of Markie, and I also have to clean up and get meals for us and talk to all the stupid people on the phone who call and ask, "How _are_ you, dear?" as if they're God and we're just some poor people who need their charity. I know it drives Mom really wild too. Markie asks for Dad all the time—he's been picking like crazy at the arm of the sofa near the TV till the material's half in shreds. And the other night he started wetting his bed. He must have been really embarrassed about it because he put all his Legos and stuff on top of the bed to try and hide it, but I could smell it a mile away. I told Mom about it, and she didn't seem to think it was such a big deal. She says he'll get over it if we don't make a fuss about it, and I should just wash the sheets. Like I haven't been doing that every morning! Anyway, why doesn't _she_ wash the sheets?

Really, Truly, Everything's Fine

Thursday, February 2

Mary Kate wanted us to go to Sheri's to make posters today, and we did, but I felt really bad about Markie because he had to go to the Carrolls' after school. Even though he likes the Carrolls fine, I know he likes it better when I come home to baby-sit him. Charlotte said he just sat with the dog and watched TV till I got there and practically wouldn't talk to anybody. I told Mom and she might (I hope, I hope!) be trying to get Grandma Rider to come after school a few days a week so I can sometimes make plans of my own. That way Markie could at least be in his own house.

Not that I have that much to do. Making posters wasn't exactly a great time. We did think of a slogan, which is RIDER/TREA$ (written like that, with a dollar sign), and everyone liked the idea of the can-sculpture show, but people still act kind of weird toward me. I can't explain it. If Mary Kate wasn't campaign manager, I bet none of them would even be helping me out. I felt bad for Mary Kate because she was trying so hard to get everyone "up" and cheerful, and then Cindy mentioned something about going to the mall this weekend and it was pretty obvious Sheri and Cindy had made plans and hadn't invited me. Mary Kate said it was the first she'd heard of it too, but I'll bet! And next week I'm going to have to give a campaign speech in front of the whole class and no one even likes me anymore! Maybe I'll just get sick and stay home from school.

I wish I knew more about what was going on. I was thinking yesterday that if Dad's a terrible thief like everyone says, then how come Mom says he doesn't have any money? And why is he staying in an apartment that just has a few pieces of furniture?

Friday, February 3

I found out today that Vanessa doesn't have any brothers or sisters. She talks about her aunt a lot, who's some kind of folk singer, and she really seems to like her. And she <u>is</u> into tarot cards, but not to tell people's fortunes particularly. She really likes the art and wants to paint herself a pack of tarot cards. She's super-talented at drawing and painting, even though she doesn't always try very hard in Mrs. Eisenstadt's class. But when she does do something, it's always amazing.

I told Mom Mrs. Maylie said I could talk to the school counselor if I wanted to, and Mom did her ice queen act and said as far as she was concerned, there was nothing to talk about, and the less everyone knows about our business, the better.

The trouble is, I think that includes me.

chapter

11

"It's show-and-tell time," Vanessa told Jill, catching her at her locker as Jill was gathering up her books for study hall. "Are you ready?" Vanessa's face was flushed, and she was carrying a long brown cardboard tube and a shiny pink box with a sign attached.

"I don't know," Jill said. "Am I going to like this?"

"Decide for yourself. Actually I have three show-and-tells. Let's go with the box first. It's my valentine box. I'm going to put it in front of my locker." She set down the mailing tube and held out the pink box to Jill. "What do you think of the sign?"

Jill read the sign, which was lettered in neat black print:

> Attention all 8th-grade guys. It's my goal
> this year to get valentines from every male
> in the class. I hope you'll all take part in this

effort. Do not be left out! To further your convenience, I will keep this box outside my locker (#330) until Valentine's Day. All you have to do is place your contribution in the slot. Thanking you in advance, Vanessa Waters.

"You wouldn't!" said Jill, wide eyed.

"Want to bet?"

Jill shook her head, laughing.

"So that's show-and-tell one," Vanessa said with satisfaction, putting down the box and picking up the cardboard tube. "Do you want to see number two?" Without waiting for Jill to answer, she pulled something out of the tube. "The story on this is that I needed some extra credits for Mrs. Eisenstadt, for getting assignments in late. She lets me do whatever I want, as long as it's an art project. So I made this for you." She unfurled a poster-sized piece of heavy paper. "It's a campaign poster," she told Jill unnecessarily.

"Oh, wow, it's awesome," breathed Jill. Somehow Vanessa had managed to sprinkle the letters for "RIDER/TREA$" across the paper so they made a kind of pattern but still spelled out the slogan clearly, and underneath the letters she'd swirled colors in a way that gave the total work an almost psychedelic effect. Jill could have looked at the poster forever.

"If you want, I can put it up in the cafeteria for you once Mrs. Eisenstadt sees it," Vanessa said.

"Don't you want to sign it or something? I mean, it's so good, it's going to make all the other posters look sick. We need to put it someplace where everyone will see it.

Maybe in the middle of that back wall near the tray tables."

"Okay, but I think there's already one there. I looked this morning." Vanessa studied her work one last time, then drew a deep breath and set the poster aside. "Anyway, you can decide where it goes," she said. "And forget about signing it. I'm not exactly a political asset. Do you want to see show-and-tell three?" She picked up the cardboard tube again. "It's another make-up assignment."

Jill looked at her watch. "I'd love to but—oh no, what happened? Did we miss the bell? I'll be late for study hall!" She frantically started gathering up her books. "You can show me your surprise at lunch, Vanessa—"

Vanessa waved her hands in front of Jill's face. "Chill, girl. No, better still, come with me." Quickly she pulled Jill around the corner into the stairwell. "What's the big deal? Just skip the study hall. I do it all the time. Who do you have, anyway?"

"Mr. Betts."

"Well, forget it, he's an old pussycat. If he asks where you were, just say you didn't feel well and were in the bathroom. That'll end it. Guy teachers are always terrified you'll wind up talking about your period."

"Vanessa!"

"Listen, I want to show you this other painting. But I want you to promise me you'll tell me what you really think of it."

Jill had never seen Vanessa so serious. And probably Vanessa was right; it was better to skip study hall than to walk in this late anyway. "Okay," she said. "I give up. Show me."

Vanessa started working on getting the painting out of the tube. "I did this a while ago," she told Jill, turning the tube upside down and thumping on it, "but Mrs. E. was so mad about my missed assignments, I brought this in for an extra, extra credit. It's bad enough to be flunking other things, but I don't want to flunk Art too."

"You could never flunk Art!" Jill told her. "You're too good."

"Yeah, well, Mrs. Eisenstadt says 'good' isn't any good in theory. She wants actual work. Like I can turn these out at a moment's notice." Vanessa pulled the painting from the tube and turned it so Jill could see.

"Oh, wow, Vanessa." Jill stared at the painting, which was rendered in flat, bright colors and utterly simple— just an empty rocking chair by a bed. Next to the bed, which was neatly made with a yellow spread, a lamp rested on a table. But it was the rocking chair that made Jill shake her head—she swore it was actually moving. It looked as if someone had just gotten up from it.

Vanessa's eyes were on Jill's face. "You like it?"

"I love it," Jill replied simply. "Really, Vanessa, it's unbelievable. Where'd you learn to paint like that?"

"My mom," Vanessa said shortly. "So anyway, that's all the show-and-tells," she added, rolling up the canvas. "How're we doing now on third period?"

"Twenty-five minutes left."

"See, what'd I tell you? Study hall's easy. I, on the other hand, am actually missing an algebra test right now."

"A test? Why didn't you say something? No wonder you're flunking!"

Vanessa shrugged and started easing the painting

back into the tube.

"It's just a test," she said. "So when do you want to put up the poster? After school?"

Jill shook her head. "There's this big meeting in the cafeteria right after school about the Valentine Dance. All the candidates are expected to be there. But they said other people are welcome too. If you come we could hang up the poster afterward."

Vanessa raised her eyebrows meaningfully.

"Well, why not? It wouldn't kill you to go to a meeting," Jill retorted.

"No, and it doesn't kill Russell the Muscle to be in art class either. It's just a total waste of time. I'll tell you what, you go do your little committee thing, and I'll take care of the poster in the morning."

"Fine." Jill hated it when Vanessa got condescending. "See you at lunch, maybe. I hope Mrs. E. gives you lots of extra credit."

"She will," Vanessa said. "I just named the chair painting for her."

Jill looked at her. "I don't get it."

"I'm calling it 'I Love You, Mrs. Eisenstadt,'" Vanessa said, grinning. "I wrote it on the back. How many extra points do you think that'll be good for?"

chapter

12

The cafeteria was buzzing when Jill arrived after school for the Valentine Dance meeting. Students milled around, waiting for the meeting to start; the dance committee was hawking tickets; and campaign posters shouted messages from the walls. Not seeing any of the people she ordinarily hung out with, Jill slipped quietly into a seat by the door.

"Anyone using this chair?" said a male voice. Startled, Jill looked up to see Micah Barnes grinning down at her. She shook her head.

"Cool," said Micah, dropping into a seat opposite her. "I need to be by the door so I can leave early." Putting his hands behind his head, he leaned back in his chair until Jill was sure he'd fall over. He had the strangest eyes— deep-set and clear, almost transparent green.

He looked at her for a moment, then cocked his head. "So," he said to Jill in his lazy voice, "you planning to actually go to this dance?"

"I don't know," Jill murmured.

"It might not be too bad. Do you know who's doing the music?"

Jill shook her head as two of Micah's friends came and sat down with him. Across the cafeteria, Jill saw Sheri and Cindy signaling to her, but she couldn't go over there now; Micah might be offended. As the meeting got under way, Jill tried to look past him at the various people who were making announcements, but Micah was hard to ignore. He kept waggling his sandy eyebrows at her and walking his fingers across the table toward the notebook she had pulled out to take notes in. When Sarah Schramm, the dance committee chairperson, announced the name of the DJ hired for the dance, Micah inhaled sharply with pleasure. "Yessssss," he said, drumming his fists on the table. Then he gave Jill a two-thumbs-up sign.

"He's great. You on?" he asked her.

Blushing, Jill shrugged.

"Hey, you need to hear him, trust me," Micah said.

Jill struggled to think of something to say. Why was she so tongue-tied? She couldn't believe Micah really cared whether she was going to the dance; probably he was just being polite. He certainly hadn't paid her any attention before. Micah and his friends were a bit on the edge—not really the popular group, but definitely cool.

Micah slipped out of the cafeteria right after the DJ announcement, and the meeting ended about fifteen minutes later. As Jill was buttoning her coat and wrapping her scarf around her neck, Cindy and Sheri came over to say hi to her.

"So what was *that* all about?" Cindy asked as they

walked out of the building together.

"What do you mean?"

"Was there something going on there with Micah, or was I seeing things?"

"I think you were seeing things."

"You going to the dance with him?"

Jill felt her face get hot. "Don't be silly, Cindy! He was just sitting there."

"Looked like more than that to me," said Cindy.

Outside the high school, Sheri's mom honked to get Sheri's attention and then offered Jill and Cindy a ride home too. Cindy said she'd called her dad to come and get her, but Jill accepted gratefully—she'd been dreading the long, cold walk to her house.

"How are you, dear?" Mrs. Leonard asked as Jill slid across the back seat. "We haven't seen you in a long time."

"I'm fine." Jill gave one last, secret glance out the car window to see if Micah might be hanging around the building, but he seemed to be long gone. "Thanks for giving me a ride."

"I hear you're running for class treasurer?"

Jill nodded.

"I thought your posters looked great," Sheri told Jill, turning around to look at her. "Mary Kate's doing a good job. How come she wasn't at the meeting?"

"This is her afternoon to volunteer at the shelter. She does that every Monday with a friend from her church."

In the front seat, Sheri started chatting with her mother about Mary Kate's efforts as campaign manager, so Jill leaned back and tried to decide whether she wanted to go to the dance. Usually she hated dances—

everyone stood around self-consciously, except for the most popular couples, who either hogged the floor with show-off moves or draped themselves on each other till it was embarrassing to watch them. But Micah had said the DJ would be really good. Why would he have said that if he wasn't secretly encouraging her to go? Maybe he even wanted to dance with her.

Yeah, right. Telling herself not to be such an idiot, Jill rubbed a circle with her mittened hand on the steamy window. Outside, the snow was turning purple, and windows in the houses near the street glowed yellow with light. "You can let me off up at the top of my driveway, Mrs. Leonard," she said. "The driveway's pretty icy and you might have trouble getting back up."

"Is this all right, dear?" Mrs. Leonard asked a few moments later, easing the car to a stop by Jill's mailbox. "You'll watch yourself walking down now, won't you? And say hi to your mom for me. How's she doing, by the way?"

"Fine," said Jill brightly, wondering if that would ever seem like a normal question again. "Busy."

"And your dad?"

"He's fine too," Jill said, quickly opening the door. The Leonards weren't friendly with her parents—why was Mrs. Leonard asking these things? "I'll tell them you said hello. Thanks again," she said, escaping from the car before Mrs. Leonard could say anything else.

Jill tried not to think uncharitable thoughts about Sheri's mother as she picked her way through the snow along the edge of the driveway—hadn't Mrs. Leonard been nice enough to give her a ride home? Jill was glad she hadn't let them drive her all the way to the end of the cul-de-sac though. Suddenly about halfway down the hill, Jill realized that there were no lights on in her house. Her heart started pounding. What was going on? Grandma Rider was supposed to be watching Markie this afternoon. Rushing to the kitchen door, Jill found a note taped on the glass in her grandmother's handwriting that said "Markie's at Carrolls'." She grabbed the note, dropped her backpack, and ran to the Carrolls'.

"What's up?" she asked Charlotte anxiously, wiping her snow-covered feet on the braided rug just inside Charlotte's kitchen door. "Where's Markie? Is everything okay?"

"He's downstairs with Keith, watching TV," said Charlotte, welcoming her inside. "Your grandmother had to leave, so she brought him here. I couldn't quite get the whole story. Both of them were pretty upset. Something about a school overnight Saturday that Markie didn't want to go to, and when your grandmother urged him to change his mind, he shut down completely and refused to even speak to her. She said he aimed the remote at her to turn her off whenever she started to talk to him."

Jill sank down onto a kitchen chair. Was she hearing right? *Markie* did that?

"Don't worry, I think Keith's got him calmed down," said Charlotte. "He's probably just upset by all the changes in your house the last few weeks. He misses his routine."

"He misses my dad, that's what!" Jill said bitterly. "Why did the newspaper have to print that dumb article anyway?"

Charlotte put a gentle hand on Jill's arm. "It's easy to blame the article, darling," she said. "But you know the newspaper didn't invent those things; at least some of what it reported was true. You can't hide from that, Jill. There's going to be a trial pretty soon, and your dad'll most likely be testifying."

"Yeah, but he told me he's not the criminal. He's helping them!"

"Oh, Jill, he's trying to get as lenient a sentence as possible. That's what plea bargains are all about."

Jill shook off Charlotte's hand. "How do you know the newspaper didn't get it wrong?" she said angrily. "Maybe my dad didn't really do what they said he did! I don't see why no one will give him a chance. Anyway, isn't a person supposed to be innocent till he's proven guilty?"

"Of course he is, darling. But your father himself said he was guilty. That was the plea he made in front of the court."

Shut up, shut up, shut up, Jill screamed silently. She could hardly breathe, her chest felt so tight. How could Charlotte, of all people, say these things to her? Tears blurring her vision, she stared blindly at some catalogs for Charlotte's stationery business strewn across the table in front of her. Charlotte got up and put her arms around her. Jill opened her mouth to speak, but no sound came out. She could only shake her head helplessly.

"Jill?" came a wavering voice from the basement play-room. And then softer, "Is Jill here?"

"I think she might be," answered Keith's soothing voice. "Let's go see."

Jill moved quickly away from Charlotte. Someone in the playroom switched off the muted crashes and bangs of Markie's beloved cartoons, and then footsteps clat-tered up the stairs and Markie burst into the kitchen and flung himself at her. His corduroys and sweatshirt were rumpled, and there was a pattern of indentations on one cheek, as if he'd fallen asleep watching television.

Keith followed him into the kitchen.

"Where *were* you?" Markie said to Jill plaintively, his voice muffled against his sister's midriff.

"I had a meeting," Jill said, wiping her eyes and kneeling down next to him. "But I got here as soon as I could."

"Can we go home, please?" whispered Markie. "I want to go home."

Charlotte's eyes met Jill's over Markie's head.

"Sure you can, Markie," Charlotte told him. "Why don't you go get your coat? I want to pack up some of Keith's sugar cookies for Jill to take home with her. Big sisters need treats too."

"Did you have cookies?" Jill asked her brother.

Markie nodded.

"Were they good?"

He nodded again.

"Dog got your tongue?"

Markie grinned faintly. Jill hugged her little brother fiercely. She felt so bad for him. How could Grandma Rider have deserted him as she did? She should have known Markie wouldn't be rude unless he was really upset about something.

Jill could feel Charlotte's concerned eyes on her, but she couldn't bring herself to look up. Sympathy right now might undermine her, might cause her to think about what she didn't want to think about. She had to stay strong, if not for her own sake, then for Markie's. Because if what Charlotte was saying was true, then where would that leave her and Markie?

Really, Truly, Everything's Fine

A sudden wave of loneliness made Jill's chest constrict. She clung to Markie. "Did you do any more Dinomans?" she asked softly.

She could feel Markie nod. "One where he saves a space alien and one where he saves Daddy. I did them before I got here. They're still in my room."

"Well, let's go check them out." Jill straightened up. "Go get your boots and jacket and say thank-you to the Carrolls for taking such good care of you."

"Thank you, Keith and Charlotte," Markie murmured obediently. "I'm sorry I got Grandma Rider mad at me."

Charlotte sent an anguished glance toward Keith, then bent down to embrace Markie. "Oh, my darling, you come anytime. We loved having you! We're just glad that we were home."

chapter

13

Monday, February 6

Sometimes I wish I'd never been nominated. Like right now, for example. I'm supposed to be memorizing my stupid campaign speech, but I keep thinking about other things and my mind just goes blank. And we can't even use notes—isn't that ridiculous? It has to be "spontaneous." (Which means write it and memorize it.) What does memorizing a speech have to do with being treasurer? I'll probably have a heart attack and die right up there on the stage.

Mom needed to work late tonight, so I had to fix dinner and get Markie to bed. It took me a while, but I think I finally figured out the reason Markie freaked out with Grandma Rider. It was the overnight. Since he's been wetting his bed lately, he was afraid he might wet his sleeping bag and then everyone would make fun of him. And Grandma Rider kept insisting he needed to go—don't ask me why. Maybe because it was a school thing, or she thought he should get out more. And if that wasn't bad enough, when Markie told her he had to stay home and work on his Dinos, she called them his silly drawings. Anyway, I just tore up the permission slip and told Markie he could do what he wanted. If Mom doesn't like it, too bad—she should have been here to decide.

After dinner Markie and I worked a lot on his project, which is turning out to be really cool. I asked Mom to pick up some poster board to mount the cartoons, which she did right away, but she only bought white, which doesn't exactly make for a super-dynamic display. So Markie and I decided to do some outlining with markers and to decorate the edges of each drawing to make everything brighter and more noticeable. I really want him to win a prize! He deserves it—his Dino strips are so totally cool for a little kid.

Later. Mom finally came home and I wish she'd stayed away! She can be such a jerk sometimes. I told her how upset Markie was at Charlotte's, and do you know what she said? She said, in this snippy voice: "I have a job, Jill, and my job pays the bills and puts food on the table and pays our health insurance, and since your father isn't likely to be earning money in the near future, you and Markie are just going to have to do the best you can." I wished I'd had a remote like Markie to turn off her ugly, whiny voice. And she even had the nerve to say that I should stop making it sound like our lives were so miserable, because she didn't want Grandma Rider and the neighbors to keep feeling they had to come to our rescue!

And then her friend Jackie called, and her voice got all sweet like nothing had ever happened and I could hear her telling Jackie how hard she was working but she thought it was going to pay off with a promotion and yes, the kids were busy with school and stuff, you know how kids are, and she didn't know and she didn't care (that was probably about Dad) and really, truly, everything's fine.

Stupidest saying of the MONTH:
"Everything's fine."

chapter

14

The night before the campaign speeches, Jill was rummaging frantically through her dresser drawers. What on earth was she going to wear tomorrow? On the way home Mary Kate had put on the pressure, telling Jill how much the little things mattered, like the outfit she chose, how she combed her hair, how many people she made eye contact with as she walked onto the stage.

"Wear red" had been Mary Kate's parting words to Jill. "You look great in red. And it's almost Valentine's Day, so you'll get the valentine vote."

The valentine vote! Jill slammed a drawer shut. Had Mary Kate completely lost it? Since when was there a valentine vote?

"I say, go naked," Vanessa had told Jill. "If you're naked, no one will care what you say. If you forget your speech, it won't matter a bit."

Jill was starting to worry that she would *have* to go

naked. She began pulling things wildly off hangers. Where was her brown skirt? Everything else she'd tried on hung on her as if she were a bag of bones. When had she lost so much weight? Her rust-colored sweater, which at least looked okay on her, had a big spot on it. She poked at the spot in disgust. Didn't Mom take anything to the dry cleaners anymore?

Not that Mom had mentioned one word about the election all through dinner tonight. Dad, on the other hand, had called a while ago with a pep talk. He'd asked about her speech and her fund-raising project and had even tried to get her to practice the talk with him on the phone. But Jill was afraid he'd want her to change something at the last minute. She'd finally gotten the speech memorized, and she'd screw up the whole thing if she had to change even one word. She remembered bitterly when Dad had been home to help her with school stuff from the start. But at least he remembered there was going to *be* an election.

Jill grabbed her rust-colored sweater and took it to the bathroom sink, where she began scrubbing at the spot with soap and water. But the area around the spot just got darker, so she couldn't tell whether the spot had come out; and the whole front of the sweater got so wet, she knew it would never dry before tomorrow. She threw the sopping sweater into the bathtub and made a half-hearted attempt at mopping up the bathroom floor with a towel, getting herself wet in the process. Peeling off her clammy jeans, she tried on her second-best khaki pants for tomorrow, but the pants legs were too short. What was wrong with her? She collapsed on her bed, over-whelmed with rage and frustration. Why couldn't anything go right? How could a person grow and shrink at the same time?

"Jill!" said Mom, standing at the door and looking around. "What on earth is going on in here? This room looks like a tornado's been through it."

"I'm looking for something to wear tomorrow," said Jill through clenched teeth. "Nothing fits. I need new clothes. Everything's too big or too short or in the laundry. Which is where I might as well be. Maybe I'll go hide in the clothes hamper for the rest of my life."

"Well, surely if we just—"

"Surely nothing!" retorted Jill in desperation. "I—" she spaced her words carefully—"need something to wear. Do you know where we put that brown skirt I bought last fall? At least maybe I could wear that with my white shirt. Except I've got a stupid hole in my brown tights, and I can't get up on that stage without tights on because everyone's going to be looking up my skirt."

"What do you mean 'on the stage'? Oh, Jill." Mom glanced around the room again. "Is the speech tomorrow? Why didn't you tell me?"

I shouldn't have to tell you, Jill wanted to spit out at her. *You should have known!* But instead she just turned her back and started rummaging through her tights drawer.

"Wait, wait, wait," said Mom. "If it's brown tights you're looking for, I think I have some that will fit you. And the skirt's in the front closet. Do you want to try the tights on? Can I press something for you?"

"I've got it covered," said Jill. "If I could just borrow the tights—"

"I'll go get them. Do you have your speech ready?"

"Yes."

"Are you pleased with it?"

Jill shrugged.

"Well, I'm sure it will be great."

"I guess."

"I'm really sorry, Jill." Mom stood in the doorway. "I can't believe I lost track of this. I mean, I know how important this is to you. It's just that . . ." She spread out her hands helplessly. "Can I at least give you a ride in the morning?"

"That's okay, Mary Kate will want me on the bus. You know Mary Kate, campaigning to the end."

Mom nodded.

"Anyway, if you could just find me those tights—"

"Sure. I'll get the skirt too. I know just where it is." Mom turned to go, then turned back again. "I *am* sorry about this, Jill."

Jill stood mute—was she supposed to say it was okay? When her mother came back with the tights and skirt, she was still in the same spot.

"Thanks," she murmured politely.

"Maybe they'll bring you luck."

Yeah, sure.

"I'm sorry, Jill."

Right, you said that.

"I think Markie wants you," Jill said as Markie called urgently from the other room.

Mom ran into the hall, and Jill sank down on her bed and buried her face in her hands. Sometimes being sorry just didn't cut it; sometimes a person needed other things too.

chapter

15

"You ready for this?" Vanessa asked Jill seventh period, as they walked to the auditorium for the speech.

"Yes. No. I don't know. What if I blow it, Vanessa? What if I get up there and make an absolute fool of myself?" Tucking in her shirt nervously, Jill noticed a spot right next to where the shirt buttoned down the front. "And now I've got a spot on my shirt!" she wailed. "What am I going to do?"

"Just button your sweater."

"I can't! It'll look dorky! Come on, help me, Vanessa! I've got to get up on the *stage*."

"Wait a minute." Vanessa put down her big black satchel and fished around in it, pulling out a bottle of Liquid Paper. "Hold still now."

"What are you going to do?"

"Cover up the spot."

"Vanessa, you're going to make a—"

"Do you want it gone or what?"

Expertly, before Jill could protest again, Vanessa painted Liquid Paper over the spot. She stood back and inspected her work. "It's a good thing you're wearing a white shirt," she muttered. "Close up's not perfect, but from a distance, no spot. I guarantee it."

"This way, Jill. All candidates in the Green Room," called Mrs. Maylie from down the hall.

"Uh . . ." Jill looked down at her shirt.

"Break a leg, girl!" Vanessa said.

Moments later Jill was sitting on a hard chair on the stage in front of all the seventh- and eighth-graders in the school, the stage lights making her perspire a little, her heart pounding till she thought she'd faint. Over and over again, through her morning classes, during lunch, through the two classes after lunch, she had been rehearsing the first line of her speech like a mantra: "I'm Jill Rider, as most of you know, and I'm asking you to vote for me and the coolest fund-raising plan this school has ever seen." Cindy and Sheri had told her to be funny, and Mary Kate had told her to be dramatic; but Jill was counting on her can-sculpture project to get people's attention and their votes. The truth was, she wasn't the politician type and never would be. But she really liked her fund-raising proposal, and she hoped other people would too—maybe enough to get her the votes she needed to be treasurer. Probably that was stupid of her, but that was the way she felt.

People were still coming into the auditorium. Jill couldn't find Mary Kate or Sheri or Cindy, though she thought she saw Vanessa leaning against the wall in the back of the room. Russell and Eric and assorted members of the football and soccer teams were lined up in the first three rows, Eric's eyes narrowed, his fox face sharp with anticipation. Russell punched Eric on the arm and Eric nodded, then gave Amy a thumbs-up sign. Amy, who was sitting next to Jill, stared straight ahead, looking almost as nervous as Jill felt.

A hush fell over the auditorium as Mrs. Maylie walked up to the podium. Jill clenched her fists, concentrating on the feel of her fingernails stabbing her palms. At least the candidates for treasurer made their speeches first. Once she'd gotten hers over with, maybe she could breathe again.

Mrs. Maylie called Amy, and Jill heard Amy's voice drift in and out of her consciousness. She watched Amy's right leg shaking, noticed that her boots were run down at the heels, that her iridescent earrings flashed pink and blue in the stage lights as she talked about making money for the treasury, selling candy, school spirit, all the usual. Russell was looking nervous, too. That was kind of nice, Jill thought. Maybe he really cared about Amy.

Jill was next. Mrs. Maylie smiled at her and called her name; Jill stood and moved automatically to the podium. "I'm Jill Rider, as most of you know," she said, her voice trembling a little, "and I'm asking you to vote for me and the coolest fund-raising . . ."

It wasn't so bad once she got started. After a sentence or two, with her voice under control, the words flowed easily. Jill talked about the can-sculpture project and the neat sculptures that had been submitted in other cities that had had shows like that—railroad trains and American flags and football stadiums, all made out of canned goods that were donated after the show to local food banks. The class could charge admission to the exhibit and keep what money they made for class expenses; they could also ask for more canned goods to be donated at the door. "So we could have fun and help feed hungry people and make money—" Jill blinked and lost her stride. In front of her, Eric and Russell and a couple of their friends unfurled large white posters with red lettering that said "Jail Rider for Trea$? NOT!" Jill's heart started pounding till she could hear thunder in her ears; her face was burning. The boys jiggled the signs up and down, taunting her. Jill couldn't concentrate. Why didn't someone make them stop?

"Jill . . . boys . . . for goodness sake!" Mrs. Maylie hurried up behind Jill. Jill had lost her place completely. She muttered some words that sounded right for the end of a speech and fled from the stage, almost tripping over Maria Juarez's feet as she ran. She tore out of the Green Room and down the polished corridor, finally ducking into the girls' bathroom at the end of the hall where she held on to the sink for support, painfully gasping in air. When she heard footsteps coming down the corridor, she ran into one of the stalls and sat motionless on the toilet, holding her feet up so no one would know she was in there.

"Jill?" came a soft voice, and she barely breathed, willing the person to leave. Finally the footsteps retreated, and the door hissed open and shut. Jill sat numbly, staring at the scratched gunmetal gray door of her stall. "Sharon Adores Tyler," someone had written in red. Below that were etched the words: "This is a Gum Door. Leave your gum here," and several people had left wrinkled pink blobs of chewed gum on the painted surface. The door and walls were a mass of graffiti; on the wall adjoining the gum deposits, someone particularly nasty had written: "Let's make an ugliest person. She would have Lisa M's nose, and Carla R's hair . . ." and then other people had added their own cruel contributions. Jill's name wasn't there, but down near the bottom, she saw that someone had added "Vanessa's hips." Jill grabbed for her backpack to find a pen or a marker to obliterate Vanessa's name—what if Vanessa used this stall?—but then she remembered she'd left her belongings in the Green Room. The only other way she could think of to keep Vanessa out of the stall was to disable the toilet. Furiously she stuffed the bowl full of toilet paper; to be extra safe, she dashed out of the stall to grab some paper towels, which she threw in as well. Then she flushed it and ran.

Halfway down the hall, her legs began shaking. What had she just done? If the toilet overflowed, the bathroom could wind up under two feet of water. Water could even drip through the ceiling and ruin the classrooms below. Was she losing her mind? Probably she'd get expelled if they found out she was the one responsible.

The halls were still deserted; apparently the assembly wasn't over yet. Jill took the long way around to the Green Room—she didn't know what she was going to do next, but she knew she needed to get her backpack. In the Green Room, she swiped hastily at her tear-stained face with a tissue and grabbed the backpack to leave. But she was too late. The other candidates burst into the room, exclaiming and chattering. They froze when they saw her.

Maria Juarez recovered first. "Are you okay, Jill?" she asked. "Mrs. Maylie's looking for you. She thinks what those boys did was awful."

Amy looked almost as upset as Jill felt.

"Don't blame Amy; she didn't know," her friend Suzy said quickly.

"Really," Amy assured Jill. "I didn't."

"Everyone was so worried about you," Suzy told Jill, but Jill didn't care what everyone else felt. What she needed desperately was space; she needed to get away.

Miraculously Vanessa appeared at the door. "Excuse us, everyone, Jill's wanted in the hall," she said. She grabbed Jill and pulled her out of the room. "Those jerks!" she fumed. "Those idiots! Those—"

She looked at Jill, who wasn't sure at this point that her knees would hold her up. "Don't give 'em an inch," she instructed Jill angrily. "Head up. Shoulders back. Let's go to Art."

"I can't, Vanessa. For one thing, Amy and Russell'll be there! I just want to go—"

"You have to." Giving her no chance to respond, Vanessa pulled her along the corridor and down the stairway to the Art Room. "It's the last class of the day. You can fall apart later. Anyway, you won't see Russell's ugly face, believe me. I think he and his buddy Eric are going to be in the office for a long, long time."

"But—"

"It's like falling off a horse. Get back on now, or you'll never ride again. Anyway," Vanessa said firmly, "I've got a diversion planned. Trust me. You can do this."

Marching into the Art Room with Jill in tow, she threw her free arm around Mrs. Eisenstadt. "Have I ever told you how wonderful this woman is?" she asked Jill. "She's my absolute favorite teacher. She's the light of my life. Will you be my valentine, Mrs. E.?"

"Okay, Vanessa, what are you up to?" Mrs. Eisenstadt said.

Jill should never have let Vanessa bring her here. Mrs. Eisenstadt was probably going to say something about the assembly, and then she'd lose it again. Already she could feel tears threatening. Panic gripped her— what if she fell apart a second time?

Looking around wildly for an escape route, she saw Angelique Ong and Graciela Moreno come into class, but they barely even noticed her; instead Angelique pointed at Mrs. Eisenstadt and whispered to Graciela, and they both burst out laughing. Mrs. Eisenstadt turned toward them, and Jill saw what the joke was; Vanessa had stuck a heart-shaped red "Kiss Me" sign on Mrs. Eisenstadt's back. Others in the room caught sight of the sign and started laughing too.

"Hey, Mrs. Eisenstadt," said Graciela, running over and kissing Mrs. Eisenstadt on the cheek. Angelique grinned self-consciously and slipped into her seat. "Way to go, Mrs. E.!" said Luis Hernandez, blowing her a kiss as he walked into the room.

"I hope you know, class, that it's in my power to keep you all from graduating," Mrs. Eisenstadt warned as more and more students surrounded her with kisses.

"It's almost Valentine's Day, Mrs. E. Get into the spirit!" Vanessa chided her. Blessing Vanessa for the distraction, Jill got her folder from the table by the windows and slipped into her seat. Taking a deep breath, she took out her collage, which was ready for its second layer. *Six large silver strips, six small red ones, keep them straight, let the glue dry. Concentrate, Jill.* Russell and Amy weren't in class yet. Only forty-five long minutes more and she'd have made it through the day.

chapter 16

The house was deserted when Jill finally got home. She pulled an old Hudson Bay blanket over her head and huddled on the sofa beneath it, knees drawn up to her chest, ignoring the ring of the telephone. When Markie arrived, she came out long enough to give him a snack, then settled him down with his drawing materials and retreated to the sofa again. Markie looked at her strangely but didn't say anything.

By the time Mom arrived home, Jill was in her bedroom, pretending to be taking a nap. "Tell them I'm sleeping," she yelled when the phone rang and her mother called her name. But then the phone rang again, and again.

"Jill?" said Mom, opening the door of her room. "Get up, please. I need to talk to you."

"I don't feel like talking. Can't it wait?"

"No, it can't." Mom sat down on her bed. "That was Charlotte on the phone. She said Mary Kate told her something happened at school today. And then Mrs. Maylie called to see how you were."

"What did you say?"

"I said you were fine. But I want to know what happened."

"Nothing. I just forgot my speech at the end. No big deal."

"Oh, Jill. Did you manage to finish?"

"I'm not still up there, am I?"

In the dim light of the room, Jill saw her mother flinch. She quickly stifled a pang of guilt. Mom was the one who should feel guilty. Why was she always the last one to know what was going on in Jill's life?

"You're sure that's all that happened?" said Mom.

"Yeah. I just blew it. Though we won't get actual results until tomorrow."

"Well, I'm sorry." Mom hesitated. "Anyway, dinner's ready. Maybe you'll feel better if you eat something."

"What's for dinner?"

"One of those casseroles. I think it's some kind of pasta."

One of the pity casseroles from the neighbors. Jill's stomach turned. "I think I'll just skip dinner," she said. "I'm not that hungry. In fact, I think I'll go take a shower now. If anyone else calls, tell them I went to bed early."

But sleep didn't come easily. By midnight Jill's sheets were in a tangle and her head was aching. She forced herself out of bed to find the thermometer, but she couldn't work up a fever. So much for not being able to go to school tomorrow. How was she going to face it? Vanessa couldn't provide diversions all day, and as soon as the election results came out, Jill knew all eyes would be on her. Maybe she should just withdraw from running for treasurer and make it easy on herself. But then people would make a big deal about that too.

The next morning on the bus, Mary Kate treated Jill like a patient, chattering about the weather and the basketball team and the present her dad was going to get her mom for Valentine's Day. Not a word about the election, which was obviously the thing that was most on her mind. It was too bizarre—it was all Jill could do not to start laughing hysterically. When the bus arrived at school, she escaped from Mary Kate and made a beeline into the building, but she couldn't bring herself to take off her jacket. Standing before her locker, she looked around quickly, then walked deliberately back outside, heart thundering wildly. Slipping behind the storage building next to the gym, she pressed close to the metal wall of the shed and stood practically without breathing. Then when everyone had gone into the school, she fled the school grounds and ran around the corner toward home.

A serious thaw the night before had sent small streams of water flowing along the sides of the road, and the snow was pockmarked by drips from the tree branches above. Slowing her pace, Jill stamped hard on a sheet of ice covering a puddle, setting the water below roiling and bubbling from the pressure. But the ice didn't break. Angrily she stamped on it again. She was sick of taking everything the world dished out to her; she refused to do that anymore. If she got in trouble for skipping school, so be it.

89

• • •

Two bags of valentine hearts sat on the kitchen table when Jill entered the house, the kind of candy with little messages written on each heart. Dad must have come after she'd left for school. The bag labeled "Jill" had a message attached to it in Dad's handwriting: "Congratulations, I'm sure."

"Yeah, well, don't be so sure," Jill muttered, dropping the bag back on the table. It slid off the edge and landed on the floor. She didn't bother to pick it up.

Although the February grayness permeated the house, Jill didn't turn on any lights, and since Mom had turned the thermostat down for the day, the house was chilly and damp. Jill wandered from room to room, unable to settle in any one place—even her own room didn't feel like somewhere she belonged. Finally, though, she lay down on her bed, rested her head on her arms, and stared at the ceiling. What on earth was she going to do with herself? What was happening to her life?

Somehow she must have slipped into sleep, because the next thing she knew the doorbell was ringing urgently, and then someone started pounding on the kitchen door. In a fog, Jill jumped up and ran to see who it was.

"Let me in; it's cold out here!" Vanessa glared at her through the door window.

Jill opened the door. How had Vanessa gotten here? How did Vanessa even know where she lived?

"Honestly, what kind of hostess are you?" said Vanessa, sweeping into the kitchen in a blast of outdoor air. "After I walked all the way here! I'll probably have to rest for a week after this!

"So," she continued, studying Jill. "You chickened out after all."

"I was asleep. I think I'm getting sick," Jill told her defensively.

Vanessa grinned wickedly. "What? With chicken pox?"

"You know, Vanessa, I don't have to—"

"Do you want to know who won the election?"

"Not particularly."

"Fine. Suit yourself."

"Okay, who?" Jill said sullenly after a moment.

"Ronna, Jonah, Luis, and Amy. Amy swears she didn't know what the guys were going to do." She hesitated for a minute. "How much do you care about losing?"

Jill sighed. "I don't know. Everything kind of stinks right now."

Vanessa nodded, then sat down at the table. "Anything good to eat in this house?" she asked. "I'm famished after that walk."

"Well, you've come to the wrong place. My mom needs to go to the store. You can have some valentine candy if you want, though. Eat from my bag, not Markie's."

Jill picked up the candy from the floor and dropped the bag on the table in front of Vanessa, who screwed up her face but opened the bag anyway. "We should have gone to my house," she said. "The food's much better there."

"Why, is your mom a good cook?"

"She was."

Jill frowned at her. "What do you mean, she 'was'?"

"I mean," said Vanessa flatly, "she was when she was alive."

"Your mom's dead?" Jill stared at her, dumbfounded. "How come you never told me?"

"I'm telling you now. She died two years ago. I don't like to talk about it, because then that's all anyone ever thinks about. Like, then I'm not Vanessa anymore—I'm the girl-whose-mother-died. You know? I mean, that's big, but people have to look past that one big thing." Vanessa laughed derisively. "I guess with me, they have to look past lots of big things. You know, someone once told me, if you're fat and you don't wear name brands, you have to be really rich to be popular. Too bad I'm not rich, isn't it? I mean, would you, Miss Perfect Person, ever have been friends with me if your dad hadn't gone flaky on you?"

"Hey, what is this? Why are you getting on *my* case?" Jill asked indignantly.

"Well, would you have been? Don't answer; I can tell you. You wouldn't have given me the time of day."

"Well, would you have tried to be friendly with me if my dad hadn't gotten into trouble, Miss I'm-Too-Above-It-All-For-Everyone?" Jill demanded. "I mean, maybe this works both ways."

Vanessa glared at her.

Jill took a deep breath. This wasn't the time to fight with Vanessa. "Anyway, I'm really sorry about your mom. I bet you miss her."

"Yeah, at least I was popular with *her*." Vanessa sighed. "Actually, believe it or not, I used to be pretty popular with other people in my old school too. Before everyone knew my mom was going to die and then people got afraid to talk to me. So I lost all my regular

92

friends, and then they made me join a support group at school. But after that, my dad and I moved. Bye-bye, support group."

"But here—"

"Here what?"

"Nothing. Never mind." What Jill had been thinking was that none of the kids here knew Vanessa's mom had died, and they still didn't want to be friends with her. Though Jill was actually surprised Vanessa was even interested in friends. Maybe that's why she'd latched on to Jill, because she'd secretly thought Jill would help her be more popular. Too bad Dad had killed that possibility too.

"My mom went ballistic when Mrs. Maylie suggested I go to a counselor," she told Vanessa. "She doesn't even like me talking to the Carrolls, who're practically family."

Vanessa shrugged. "So what if your mom gets mad at you? Do you always do what she says?"

"Yeah, right, like she knows I'm sitting here in the house on a school day."

"You mean—?" Vanessa's eyes widened, then she grinned and raised her hand to give Jill a high five. "Way to go, Jill baby!"

"It's not like I'm this big rebel . . ."

"That's for sure."

"Or that I'm going to skip school all the time."

"Did I say anything?"

"I mean, I'm me, Vanessa. I'm not you."

"Don't we both know it," said Vanessa, helping herself to another handful of valentine candy.

93

chapter

17

Friday, February 10

Boy, did I feel like an idiot when I found out about Vanessa's mom. But how was I supposed to know if she never told me? The way she talks, you'd think it wasn't that big a deal. I bet it is though. I don't know what I'd do if one of my parents died. I used to think it would be the worst thing, but now I'm not so sure. (I wouldn't tell that to Vanessa.) I know this is really terrible, but at least dying is something you can be sad about and then get over. You wouldn't have this horrible feeling like I do that something else could blow up on you at any minute.

And I just thought of another thing—if Dad has to go to jail or something, does that mean he and Mom are going to split up for good? If I had a husband, I don't know if I'd divorce him if he got into bad trouble, but he'd sure better tell me about it. Because when people lie to you, they take away your right to decide on your own how you feel about things, and I think that stinks. And it makes you a liar too. Like when Dad lies to me and then I wind up lying to Markie and my friends because I didn't get the real story on what was going on. I don't know what I'm supposed to tell Markie if Dad actually does wind up in jail. I'm worried he won't ever trust me either.

Vanessa says she remembers what it felt like when her mom died, not having any privacy and everyone thinking they had a right to mind her business. And I know exactly what she means. I wonder what she was like before her mom died. I can't believe she wore those weird clothes and skipped school and was sarcastic about everything the way she is now, especially since she said she used to be popular. I hope I don't change that much. People think I'm already different, and I doubt I could ever go back to being the old Jill, which I know wasn't perfect but at least I was pretty happy most of the time. I wonder if I'll ever be happy like that again. I mean, life can't be all about my dad forever, can it? And now that the election's over and I can just lay low for a while, maybe people'll go on to something else.

Yeah, right, Jill.

I guess Vanessa must trust me a lot or she wouldn't have told me about her mom. I don't know if I trust her a hundred percent though. Sometimes I think she's using me, that she gets some kind of charge out of twisting things around to make me do weird stuff, and she sticks with me because I'm the only friend she can get. She says her theory is that you have to stick out your tongue at everyone who's bad to you and get on with your own life. I'm not really like that, but I guess she still thinks I'm okay.

Actually, I wouldn't mind having some of my old friends back. I mean, I wouldn't necessarily stop being friends with Vanessa, but I kind of miss hanging out like a regular person.

Saturday, February 11

Stupid saying of the day: "The Lord never gives us more than we can bear."

Grandma Rider said that to Mom this morning, and let me tell you, it didn't go over big. Apparently Grandma Rider also told Mom we should work out other arrangements for taking care of Markie after school, since it didn't look like Dad would be back any time soon. I think it really stinks that she said that. I mean, it wasn't like Mom ever planned to use her as a permanent baby-sitter. And it wasn't like she did such a great job the few times she stayed with Markie either.

I've got tons of homework this weekend. I'm taking a break now, but it can't be for long. I hope the Lord didn't give me more than I can get done by Monday.

Monday, February 13

I played hooky again this afternoon, which if I keep it up is probably going to get me in trouble. I'm not like Vanessa—getting in trouble makes me nervous. On Friday I told Mom I didn't feel well, so she wrote me an excuse, but today might not be so easy. Vanessa and I cut out around two o'clock and took a bus to the mall, which if I hadn't been so scared we'd get caught, would really have been fun. Because guess who else was skipping school! Micah! I bet he was surprised to see _me_! Here's how it happened. The pet store had a parrot on display who did nothing but laugh and laugh like it had just heard the most hysterically funny thing in the world. And every single person who heard him started laughing too. So Vanessa and I decided to sit on a bench a few stores away and watch the laughers. And who should walk by but Micah. He came over and said something to me

like "you're smiling," and I said something brilliant like "so?"
So then he said I always looked so sad and I should smile
more because I looked pretty when I smiled! I didn't ask
what he was doing there, and he didn't ask what we were
doing there, but he stayed and talked for a few minutes.
Vanessa didn't say so, but I think even she thought Micah
was pretty cool. I might go to the Valentine Dance now, but
probably not. Maybe I'll just see what happens if I bump
into Micah at school.

Vanessa said she's gotten 17 valentines in her box so
far (a few of them rude), but practically none of them are
signed. I bet she wouldn't mind getting a really nice valentine, but how would she know it was a real one? (Maybe
that's the point.) Not that I've gotten even one single card
myself, but it's not officially Valentine's Day till tomorrow, so
I can still hope. Wouldn't it be weird if one of Vanessa's
valentines was from Micah?

Tuesday (Valentine's Day)

No valentines worth talking about. Unfortunately.
But I did see Micah after third period and after fifth period
and he nodded at me both times.

Tomorrow's the hobby show. Markie and I spent a
lot of time after school finishing his display so Mom can
drive all his stuff to school tomorrow. Markie and I are going
to the show for the opening, but there's some big meeting at
the hospital that Mom has to go to, so she can't be there till
the second night. Keith and Charlotte are going to go that
night too, and Mom will pick up Grandma Rider. Markie's
left a bunch of messages for Dad to come tomorrow, but we
don't know yet if he will. I'm not sure I even want him to be
there—how weird is that going to be? I showed Vanessa
some of Markie's cartoons when she was here Friday, and

she was really impressed.

Mrs. Maylie called Mom and left a message for Mom to call her, but I erased it. I hope it wasn't about skipping school. I unplugged the phone for a while and got the answering machine light blinking so it looks like something went wrong with it, and if anyone asks, I can say we didn't get the message. Maybe Mrs. Maylie will just give up and forget about it.

chapter 18

"Markie, look!" Jill rushed across the gym to Markie's Dino-man display. "You won a ribbon! A red ribbon!"

"Is that on my Dinos?" asked Markie excitedly, running up behind her.

"It sure is!" Jill bent down to hug him. "Wow, wait till Mom finds out!"

"Are you Markie's sister?" asked a small, spiky-haired woman, coming up to the two of them. She held out her hand to Jill and looked around. "I'm Mrs. Colonna, Markie's teacher. Is your mom or your dad here?"

Jill straightened up. "Uh . . . not yet," she said. "I'm Jill."

"You've got to be so proud. Markie's really awfully talented." Mrs. Colonna turned to Markie. "I even have a special ribbon for you to wear so everyone knows who you are!"

She pinned the ribbon on to Markie's T-shirt.

"I didn't know I was going to win a prize," Markie told Jill happily.

Jill and Markie stood admiring the Dino-man posters for a few minutes, then went to check out the other entries. Markie got lots of attention because of the ribbon on his shirt, and Jill beamed at everyone who came up to congratulate him. A few people asked for Mom, but no one mentioned Dad at all. Then, just when Jill decided Dad wasn't going to make an appearance, she spotted him coming through the doorway on the far side of the gym.

"Markie," she whispered, tugging at his arm. Markie saw Dad, let out a cry, and ran across the room to him. Jill watched as Dad caught Markie up in a triumphant hug, then set him down and went with Markie to admire his exhibit.

Slowly Jill went over to join them.

"Isn't your brother great? Isn't he the best?" Dad said to Jill. "We always knew old Dino-man was a winner!"

"Daddy said he came specially to see me," Markie told Jill, holding tightly to his father's hand.

"Well, you and Dino-man," said Dad, ruffling Markie's hair.

"And he wants to take you and me out for sundaes," Markie told Jill. "To celebrate!"

Jill looked at her watch. "I don't know, Markie. Mom's supposed to pick us up at nine. She's in a meeting now, and I don't even know if I can reach her."

"Can't you leave her a message?" Markie begged. "Please, Jill, I want to. Dad says we can order anything we want."

"Just call your mother and say you have a ride," Dad told Jill. "I'll drop you off at the house when we're finished. She won't mind—it'll save her a trip."

The ice-cream parlor was noisy and crowded, but Dad insisted on staying. Jill was grateful when they finally got a seat and put in their orders. Markie was going to be exhausted tomorrow, but it was probably worth it if he was happy tonight—he'd been through so much lately. And it felt like old times—the three of them sitting at the small, marble-topped table and digging into gooey ice-cream sundaes. Jill realized how much she'd actually missed having her father around. Markie, as always, had to take a taste of everyone's sundae and decided that his own Rocky Road was best.

Dad and Markie sang songs on the way home while Jill relaxed in the back seat. "Okay, guys, it's a school night," Dad said, pulling the Jeep up next to the house. "Back to reality. See you next—"

The kitchen door slammed, and Mom came tearing out into the driveway. "Jill, Markie, I want you in the house this minute!" she ordered furiously. "Where in the world have you been? I've been sitting here pulling my hair out. I could kill you for this, Dave! Couldn't you at least have had the decency to call me?"

"Hey, whoa, hold on a minute. Jill did call you. I heard her myself. She left word on your voice mail—"

"Jill left word that she and Markie had a ride," Mom said, her voice tight with rage. "She didn't say with whom! I expected them home an hour ago! The hobby show was supposed to be over at nine. And Jill's cell phone didn't answer, and I've been phoning the school since nine fifteen and no one was there either! I've been sitting here for an hour imagining all kinds of terrible things—"

Mom's voice got higher and higher, and her face was getting red. Jill climbed quickly out of the Jeep and came around to get Markie, who had clapped his hands over his ears. "I'm sorry, Lib," said Dad. "I didn't know Jill had turned her phone off, and I didn't think there was a rule about taking my own kids out for ice cream. And to be honest, it wasn't that long. What could you possibly think had happened to them?"

"I had no idea!" Mom spat out. "Life's not so simple around here anymore, remember? Maybe you've got faith in those criminals you've been hanging around with, but I'm not as trusting as you are!"

"Quit being nuts, Lib. This is ridiculous! Do you think for one minute I'd let someone hurt our children? What do you think I am?"

"I don't *know* who you are anymore! All I ever get from you are stories and lies and excuses. I just want you out of here!" Mom was practically screaming now. "Leave! Go! Now!"

Markie looked terrified.

"Come on, Markie," said Jill gently. "Let's go inside."

"I don't want to go inside, I want to go home with Daddy! I don't like it when Mommy's mad at him!"

"It's all right, Markie," said Dad. "Mommy will calm down in a minute."

"I will not calm down!" Mom snapped at him. "Not until you turn around and get your bloody Jeep out of this driveway. Come on, Markie, you're coming with me. Jill, will you help your brother down?"

"But I don't want—" wailed Markie.

"It's okay, Markie," Jill whispered to him. "Let's go inside. Daddy needs to leave now."

"But—"

"Come on, Markie," Jill said firmly. She helped her brother out of the Jeep and ushered him into the house. Mom pulled the door shut behind them and fastened the chain latch, then stood listening for a moment as Dad started the Jeep and roared up the driveway.

"Mom?" Jill said, holding a trembling Markie beside her.

Mom opened her mouth to speak, but nothing came out.

"*Please,* Mom . . . ?"

Mom shook her head at Jill helplessly; then, shoulders shaking, she sat down, buried her face in her hands, and burst into tears.

chapter

19

Thursday, February 16

    *I couldn't write last night because I was too upset.
And today I had a horrible headache all day.*

    *It was forever till we all got to bed last night. I think
Mom was really panicked when we didn't get home from the
show on time. I almost felt sorry for her, she was so upset,
but I felt sorrier for Markie and me. I also don't know
whether I should be scared or not. Dad said there's nothing
to worry about, but how am I supposed to know whether to
believe him? He can't be sure about that! Someone should
have warned us anyway that the people he got into trouble
might try to get back at him. Mom told me last night that
was actually one of the reasons she made him move downtown, because she was worried they might come to the house
and hurt us or something. The least she could have done
was tell us! I mean, what if a stranger came up to me and
asked me to get in his car because something had happened*

to Mom or Dad? I probably wouldn't have gone, but what about Markie? Nobody warned him either.

Charlotte says I shouldn't let myself become a victim of what Dad did, that I should be sure and ask for help if I need it. But the only help I want right now is a ticket to Arizona for me and Markie. Mom can get her own ticket. Mom says there's probably going to be another article in the paper on Monday when this big jewel thief's trial begins, so I guess Charlotte was right about what's going on, even though Dad didn't say one word about it the whole time we were together last night. I wonder if he was ever planning on telling me. School's going to be so awful when all of this gets back in the paper. I don't know if I'm going to be able to stand it.

chapter

20

Sunday night Jill dreamed she blew up all the city's newspapers. She sneaked into the offices and wired the printing presses and watched the presses explode, *bam, bam, bam!* With each blast she felt immeasurably lighter. She was about to run downtown and shout to her father that he was free, that he could come back home, when suddenly she went icy with fear. She'd forgotten the radio and TV stations, and she had no more explosives to destroy them! She began rushing wildly from TV station to TV station to beg the anchor-people to leave her family alone, to kill the story; but they were all in glass booths and couldn't hear her no matter how hard she pounded on the walls. She fell to her knees weeping helplessly, her fists sliding silently down the glass.

When she awoke, she was rigid with dread; the house was quiet, the clock read 5:00 A.M. She shot up in bed and shook her arms and legs violently to wake up fully, then walked around her room in an effort to push the dreams back into the night. The images dissipating, she made herself get back into bed, but she lay there gritty-eyed in the darkness, watching her window for signs of daylight, too frightened to go back to sleep. But despite all that, there was no article in the paper that morning. In fact, Jill had a more or less normal school day—even, at times, a good one. She had a tense moment after lunch, though, when Mrs. Eisenstadt approached her in the hall—had the office heard something about the trial?

"Are you going to class? May I walk with you for a moment?" the art teacher asked Jill.

"Sure," said Jill, who was heading for Math. What else could she say? Mrs. Eisenstadt had red paint down the front of her fuzzy gray sweater. Jill wondered if she knew about it.

"I wanted to talk to you about your can-sculpture proposal," Mrs. Eisenstadt told her. "I was impressed with the way you mapped that out. I've been thinking it would be a great spring project for all the seventh- and eighth-graders. I was going to have a sculpture unit anyway, and this way the school could also help out a good cause. Would you mind if we appropriated your idea? I mean, your class is going to raise money some other way, aren't they?"

"Yeah, I think they're going to sell candy. But it's not really my idea, Mrs. Eisenstadt. Vanessa saw a show like that in New York somewhere. You should probably ask her instead."

"Well, I could do that. But you're the one who thought about putting the idea into action. So what I'd really like is for you to head a student committee to help

107

me with the show part of the project. Maybe you could ask Vanessa to help with that." Mrs. Eisenstadt grinned at Jill conspiratorially. "That is, if you can manage to get her to be on a committee."

Jill hesitated. Mrs. Eisenstadt was so nice, but maybe she wasn't fully aware of all the problems in Jill's life. "Are you sure you want me to do it?" she asked. "I mean, if you'd rather get someone who's more popular right now, you might be better off. . . ."

"Jill," said Mrs. Eisenstadt. "I know when I'm well off. And it's you I'm asking. Vanessa can definitely help, but organizational skills, as you may have noticed, are not her strong suit. And the class officers will be focused on Snickers and M&M's. So if you want to do it . . ."

Jill wanted to. Not only was she interested, she was thrilled. She really believed her idea could work, and maybe this would be a way to get herself back into school life again.

She shrugged. "Okay," she told Mrs. Eisenstadt. "If you're sure you want me."

"Good," said Mrs. Eisenstadt. "And think of a few other people besides Vanessa who might be helpful too. We'll get together next week and divide up duties. I'd like to get going as soon as we finish this collage unit."

Jill was actually in a good mood by the time she got home. She'd talked to Mary Kate on the bus, and Mary Kate had signed up immediately to help. Jill had a million ideas buzzing around in her head to make the show a success. Letting herself into the house, she went over to switch off the radio, which Mom had left playing so that it would seem as if someone were home. In the split second after she turned it off, though, she realized the announcer had said "Rider." Frantically she switched the radio back on, but the announcer was already on the next item.

The phone rang, and Jill grabbed it.

"Is this the Rider residence?" asked a female voice.

"Who's calling?"

"I just want to talk to you for a moment. Is this the Rider daughter?"

Jill didn't answer.

"Hello? This is Ann McDonald of WDRE—"

Jill slammed down the phone. This was her nightmare come to life. Why was this happening? Were reporters going to surround the house? Would they bother Markie when his bus came? Should she call Charlotte? Or Mom?

The phone rang again. Jill jumped, her heart thudding in her chest. This time she checked the caller ID. It was her mother, on the car phone.

"Good, Jill, you're home. . . ."

Jill could barely speak.

"I'll be there shortly. I've got Markie. I phoned and picked him up at school. Has anyone been calling the house?"

"Just one person," Jill managed to choke out. "Some TV lady."

"Well, check the caller ID from now on. They've been hounding me at work all day. With my luck, your dad's going to cause me to lose my job too. Don't talk to anyone, okay?"

"Did something awful happen at the trial?" Jill was holding the receiver so tightly, her hand felt numb.

"We'll talk when I get home. Just don't answer the phone till I get there."

"Is Markie all right?"

"He's fine. We've got his hobby show exhibit with us. Just lock the door, Jill, and I'll be home as soon as I can."

Jill's heart began thudding again. "Why? Who do you think might be coming? Should I call the Carrolls?"

"Everything's fine. Just sit tight. I'll be home in ten minutes."

chapter

21

"Look, Jill!" said Markie, bursting into the house.
"Dino-man's home!"

"Good, I missed him," said Jill, looking anxiously over
Markie's head at her mother.

"You helped me win the prize," Markie said. "I'm going
to put the ribbon on the refrigerator so you can see it too."

The phone rang. Mom checked the caller ID, then
didn't answer it. The ringing stopped but immediately
began again. Mom reached for the phone and turned off
the ringer, then hung up her coat and said she was going
to her room to finish some work.

"Will you look after Markie?" she asked Jill.

Jill stared at her. Did Mom really think she could leave
without telling her what had happened at the trial? She
ran down the hall after her.

"What's going on?" she said, looking back over her
shoulder at Markie.

Mom turned wearily. "Did you hear any broadcasts?"
Jill shook her head.

"Well, all I know is what the radio said. Apparently Dad's testimony against this Mr. Strade took most of the day. And on the stand Dad admitted actually stealing things from people's houses. He hadn't told me that before, so I guess that qualifies as news," Mom said bitterly.

Dad admitted what? Jill couldn't speak. Had Dad been straight-out lying to her all this time?

"I'm sorry, Jill," Mom said. "I wish you didn't have to know all this."

I'm sorry! Jill was suddenly filled with rage. If she heard that word "sorry" one more time, she was going to scream. All it meant when people apologized these days was that they were sorry she'd found out something! And what she'd found out now was that her own father was a thief. An actual thief! How could he have lied to her all these weeks about what he'd done and then let her find out by hearing it on a news broadcast? She never wanted to see him again! He deserved to go to jail! She hoped they put him in jail.

"Mommy? Jill?" called Markie, interrupting. "Where are you? I need someone!"

"Could you please help him?" Mom said to Jill, her voice rising slightly with panic. "I've got to get this report done. It's really important; it's a proposal for re-doing the whole hospital computer system. I just threw everything into my briefcase, but if I don't have it ready when the board meets in two weeks . . ."

"Yeah, sure. Okay." Jill actually felt bad for her mother. Mom didn't deserve this—none of them did.

"Mommy? Jill?" Markie called again.

Gritting her teeth, Jill turned.

"Jill?" said her mother. "Maybe we can talk later?"

Now, later, what did it matter? Right now Jill would give ten years of her life to be able to fall into a hole and come out the other side, in another country, another universe, where all her problems would be different ones. Let her mother hide in her room: What would happen would happen. Pasting a smile on her face, Jill let her feet march her back to her little brother in the kitchen.

It was weird not having the phone ring all night, but Mom refused to turn it back on. She also shut the blinds and covered the kitchen door window with an old sheet, ignoring the occasional chiming of the doorbell. She and Jill drifted through the house like ghosts all evening, afraid to say anything in front of Markie, though it was evident from the way he trailed after them that he sensed something was wrong. On the eleven o'clock news, after he was in bed, Jill and Mom listened to clips of Dad talking in clear, unambiguous language about burglary and bugging telephones and framing people. They sat on the sofa in silence, unbelieving.

Tuesday morning the story hit the papers.

Jill read the article about her father carefully three times before she went to school. Last time she'd dismissed the newpaper stories as lies; this time she wanted as many details as possible. Her father, the writer said, had used his access to the houses of his burglar-alarm customers to identify jewelry and other valuables that some man named Paul Strade then arranged to steal. Sometimes, Dad admitted, he had even stolen the things himself. Paul Strade was the kingpin, the one the FBI really wanted to get evidence against, so the FBI offered Dad a deal if he'd help them catch Strade and put him in jail. The trial that was going on now was Mr. Strade's trial, and Dad was testifying against him. In exchange Dad's punishment would be lighter. The article didn't say what that punishment would be though.

"Are you about ready for school?" Mom asked Jill, coming into the kitchen to pour coffee in her thermos before leaving for work. "Did you eat something?"

"I tried." Jill looked at the piece of toast growing cold in front of her. "How about you?" she asked her mother.

"Just coffee." Mom didn't look so good this morning. Her cheeks were hollow, and the stitch between her eyebrows was pulled tighter than Jill had ever seen it.

"What do you think's going to happen now?" Jill asked.

"I'm not sure. I guess when this trial is over, they'll sentence that Strade man, and then there'll be a sentencing hearing for Dad, since he's already pleaded guilty. They'll probably give him a lighter sentence for cooperating with them, but I doubt they'll let him off entirely. He may well have to go to jail." Mom glanced down the hall toward Markie's bedroom. "Let's cross that bridge when we come to it, okay?" She took a deep breath and looked at her watch. "I've really got to go, Jill, and so do you. But I'll try and get home early if I can."

"That's okay," Jill said. "I'll be here to watch

Markie." She hesitated. "*Why* did Daddy steal that stuff, Mom?"

Mom shook her head. "I've asked myself that same question over and over. And honestly I have no idea. Except he never was good with the truth, and he always kind of felt like the world owed him a living. And I guess he didn't think other people's rules applied to him."

Jill's eyes widened. "You knew that before this?"

Mom's eyes filled unexpectedly with tears. "Jill, really. I can't deal with this right now."

And I'm not sure I can deal with it ever! But Jill doubted she herself could stand any more truth this morning, and she knew her mother had to leave. Mom was hoping for a promotion, she had told Jill, because without Dad's income they really needed the extra money. And meeting this deadline was critical.

Jill got up from the table and dumped her toast down the garbage disposal. "Good luck with your deadline," she told her mother.

"Good luck to us all," Mom said heavily, heading down the hall to get Markie.

It was déjà vu, Jill thought, climbing on to the bus, but at least this time she knew what to do: look straight ahead, keep her expression impassive, walk quickly by anyone she knew, and flee each class the minute it was over so teachers couldn't approach her with sympathy and advice. That plan got her through the day until she went to her locker just before the last bell and found that someone had taped a copy of the trial article to her locker door. The pain that had been knotting in her neck since breakfast shot immediately to her head, making her wince. She shut her eyes briefly to try and regain her composure. *Not a big deal*, she told herself. *You've already seen the article. Someone's just being a jerk.* Opening her eyes, she looked around. Eric, a short distance down the hall, grinned at her. Jill began to hyperventilate.

"Cool, I thought I'd find you here," Vanessa's voice said behind her. Then she saw the article. Furious, she tore it off the locker. "Those—" she muttered. She spun around. "Hey, nice going, Eric," she yelled. "What are you doing, starting a free clipping service?"

Eric approached, Russell and Tobiah Holland two steps behind him. Jill struggled to slow her breathing.

"What's it to you?" Eric said to Vanessa. "Are you, like, her bodyguard or something?"

Vanessa looked at Russell. "Talk about bodyguards. Don't you have anything better to do, boy toy?"

"Hey, who you talking to, you oversized—!"

"What's going on?" interrupted Louis Dixon, coming down the hall with Bobby Barrano. "Are we missing a fight?"

"Nah," said Vanessa. "Russell and Eric here are just experiencing the normal hostilities of preadolescence. It happens to boys that age. They'll outgrow it."

"You are so stupid, girl!" Russell spat out. "You are so ugly—"

"See what I mean?" Vanessa said calmly. "Anger and insults are just the reverse side of frustration, which everyone knows is—"

Jill couldn't bear it any longer. She knew Vanessa was trying to defend her, but she was just making things worse. "I've got to go," she said hoarsely. "You can stay if you want to, Vanessa, but—"

"You heard the woman," Vanessa told the guys, doing a quick about-face. "Clear a path. We need to catch a bus."

"Where are you heading, over to the courthouse?" Eric called after Jill as she fled down the corridor toward the front door of the school.

chapter

22

Thursday, February 23

Stupid saying of the century: Maybe people'll go on to something else.

—Myself, Diary, February 10

Well, according to the 11 o'clock news, the jury is deciding right now whether this Strade guy is guilty. The next thing is that some judge will decide about Dad, but I don't know when that will be. Mom says it'll be a judge because Dad's already admitted he's guilty, so you don't need an actual trial with a jury, just someone to do the sentencing. She also keeps reminding me that Dad might go to jail. I don't know what's going to happen to us all if he goes to jail. Will we have to go visit and like, sit on the opposite side of a window and talk through the glass? And if Mom doesn't want to visit him, how will we get there? I don't want to go to some horrible jail all alone.

I'm also worried about what will happen to Dad if

he goes to jail. Jails are supposed to be awful places where people can gang up on you and there are riots sometimes and maybe even prisoners get murdered. And the Strade guy and his gang are going to be really out to get Dad. Do you think at least they'll put them in different jails?

Friday, February 24

Well, the verdict for the Strade guy was guilty, but they won't decide his sentence for another six weeks! Couldn't he run away or something by then? The paper said he could get fifteen years in prison! I think what he did was a lot worse than what Dad did though—I hope so. But when are we going to find out? I can't stand it that everything takes so long. I've had like this major headache all week, and even Advil doesn't make it go away.

Speaking of Advil, Vanessa is really nuts. I mean, she's so crazy. Today in Art I asked her if she had any Advil (which she wouldn't be allowed to give me anyway, but I was about to die from my headache and Vanessa doesn't usually care about what she's allowed to do), and she said she didn't, but then she asked Russell (!!!!) if he had any he could give me. And he said he didn't but why, did I have a headache? And Vanessa said, "No, she has cramps!" And Russell actually blushed! I mean, he turned this practically maroon color, and then Vanessa said out loud, "Look, everyone, Russell's blushing. Cramps, Russell, cramps! Tampons! Tampons!" And Russell just put his head down on the table, and Amy was patting his shoulder (but she was actually laughing too).

Monday, February 27

Markie's still wetting his bed a lot. And Friday Mrs. Colonna sent Mom a note saying he was running *around the playground at recess yelling and screaming—was something going on at home? Well, duh! Anyway, I decided that since it's worse for me when no one tells me anything, it's probably worse for Markie too, so I sat him down when he got home from school today and told him everything I know. Like, I told him straight out that Dad had admitted he stole things (but I told Markie I knew Dad was sorry, even though I don't really know that) and that he'll probably have to go to jail. And do you know what Markie said? He said, then who's going to clean my fish tank?*

Why is it grown-ups don't ever notice things? Or I guess maybe they notice, but then they drop them without doing anything about them. Like, I bet Mrs. Colonna never calls Mom if Mom doesn't answer the note (which she won't). And Mrs. Maylie never called back after I didn't give Mom her message.

Tuesday, February 28

No article in the paper!!!

Wednesday, March 1

So much happened today I don't know where to start. After lunch Vanessa and I walked by the cafeteria, and Sheri and Cindy were just walking out. And Sheri looked at Cindy and said something like, "Look, Jill, I'm really sorry about all that stuff about your dad. But it's not your—I mean, my mom says—" and then she got really pink in the face and said, "What I mean is, do you maybe want to come over this afternoon?" Apparently she and Cindy and Angelique were going to get together, and she said I should come because I hadn't hung out with them in a long time. So then I guess I must have looked at Vanessa before I answered because Sheri said, "She (meaning Vanessa) can come too if she wants." And I didn't know what to do, because it sounded a lot like Sheri's mom had made her ask me, and I didn't want any pity party from anyone. So I said maybe we could do it some other time, but I had to go home and watch Markie, which was true, but they kind of walked away mad.

So then Vanessa asked, "Was that because of me? Did you say no because of me?" I mean, did you ever hear anything so paranoid? I asked her why would I do that, and she said something about how she wouldn't exactly fit in over there, and that made me feel like smacking her. I mean, she wouldn't fit in, but that's because she tries as hard as she can <u>not</u> to fit in. Which would be all right if she didn't want to be popular, which she says she doesn't, but I think she really does! I think she just got jealous that Sheri and Cindy were trying to be friendly with me again. So then when I told her I really did have to watch Markie and it didn't have anything to do with her, she said in this gotcha tone, "What if you had a party? Would you invite me?" And I said yes, because I would, and she said, "Even a boy-girl party?" And I said yes again, and she said, "Let's see. Do it now." And then I <u>really</u> didn't know what she was talking about, because I'm not <u>having</u> a party, and I told her that, and she said "Oh, yes, you are!" and she turned around and told this bunch of kids by the cafeteria door that they were invited to a party at my house Friday night! And one of them just happened to be Micah!

Like, what was I supposed to do? I tried to tell them I couldn't do it that night because I didn't even know if my mom was going to be home, and Micah's friend Ric said, all the better, just don't tell her. He said I didn't have to worry, they'd bring food and Cokes and things like that, and they'd ask a few more kids. So at that point I just couldn't get out of it. They (I mean Micah) even said they'd bring a CD player and some cool CDs! So I guess I'm having a party. I need to tell Mom though. She's going to go ballistic, but I don't care.

Thursday, March 2

I still haven't gotten up the nerve to tell Mom, but I know I have to. Vanessa's been bugging me about it—she's really excited. She even asked me today what I thought she should wear. Do you believe it? This is Vanessa we're talking about! It's a little weird that I don't know who else is coming. (So I guess I couldn't cancel it if I wanted to, because how would I know who to tell not to come?) I know Mary Kate is busy, because it's Keith and Charlotte's anniversary tomorrow night and they're all going out to dinner, but I don't know if anyone even asked Cindy and Sheri. Of course I know Micah's coming. At least I think (hope) so. Micah's so cute—he always raises his eyebrows and looks kind of amused when he sees me, as if he knows some secret about me.

I've made up my mind—I'll tell Mom about the party at breakfast. She's got to say yes, doesn't she?

chapter 23

"I can't believe you made a commitment like that without asking me!" Mom told Jill the next morning. Mom took a sip of coffee, grimaced, and set the mug back down on the kitchen table. "What on earth were you thinking?" she demanded. "You know better than that!"

Jill dug her fingernails into her palms. She was standing with her back to the counter, too tense to sit down. "I explained to you," she said. "I didn't really *do* anything. Stuff just sort of happened." She took a deep breath. "But all the plans are made, and everyone's going to freak out if I cancel now. Please, Mom, all you have to do is be here! Couldn't you do that for me just one time?"

"You don't understand, Jill. It's the worst possible week. Half our people are in Chicago at a conference, and I'm up to my ears on that big proposal I told you about. Couldn't we at least switch it to another night?"

"I'm telling you, it's too *late* to do that—everyone's

bought the food and everything. Please, Mom, I'll do anything you ask. I'll clean the house! I'll baby-sit Markie! I won't ask for my allowance for a month! I *have* to have this party, Mom! Everyone will hate me if I don't!"

Jill could hear her voice getting whiny, but she didn't care. Mom had to say yes—she *had* to! Tears came to her eyes. "Please, Mom," she begged. "You don't have to do anything else for me all year!"

"It's not that . . ." Mom shook her head, as if to get rid of an unwelcome thought.

Jill waited, silent, afraid to say anything.

Mom pushed back her chair. "I really wish you hadn't done this, Jill."

Jill's heart was pounding in her ears.

"I guess maybe I could manage," Mom said reluctantly. "I don't know. If you were to keep Markie busy all day tomorrow, I suppose I could try and put in a full day's work and make up for lost time. But don't do this to me again, all right?"

Jill's knees went weak. "I won't, Mom, I promise. I'll do anything you say. Oh, thank you, thank you, thank you. I don't know what I would have done if you'd made me cancel!"

Jill couldn't wait to tell Vanessa. She felt like singing all day at school, she was so relieved and grateful to her mother. But then when she got to the house after school, Mom phoned and said she wasn't going to make it home after all.

"I've tried everything I can not to have to do this," she told Jill through a crackle of static on the cell phone. "I even called my assistant in Chicago to see if she could get home sooner. It just can't be helped, Jill. The computers are down in the pharmacy, and we've got to get them working again or the medications are going to get screwed up. I was thinking though—maybe Keith or Charlotte could stand in for me. Why don't you try calling them? I'm sure they'll help if they can. You know I hate to ask favors, but under the circumstances . . ."

"I don't think they can." Jill started to explain about their anniversary. "They—"

"Well, I don't know what the alternative is then. I'm afraid you'll just have to cancel the party." There was a silence. "Maybe some other time, Jill—"

"I hate you," Jill said, then hung up. She stood for a moment staring at the phone, feeling as if she might break into a million splintery pieces. Maybe, she thought bitterly, she already had one of those shards in her heart, like that character in the fairy tale.

It was pitiful that there was no one she could think of to call for advice. If she called the Carrolls, they might offer to change their plans, and she didn't want them to feel obligated. Vanessa would tell her not to cancel, but Vanessa was so hot to have the party that her advice would be worthless. Ric might be able to divert the party to someone else's house, but he was new at school and Jill didn't even know his last name. She guessed she could call Micah, but she'd rather die than do that.

She still hadn't made a decision by the time Markie came home. Which she guessed meant the party was on. Well, fine—let Mom get mad at her! By the time she got home, it would be too late to do anything about it.

Jill switched on all the lights in the house to try to make it look welcoming—a house at the end of a cul-de-sac wasn't the ideal place for a party. Maybe she should go up the drive and put balloons and a ribbon on the mailbox (not that she had any balloons) or perhaps some kind of sign. But would that just look dorky? She didn't want people to think she was clueless about parties, even if she was.

"Jill," Markie called plaintively from down the hall. "My room smells."

Oh no, had she forgotten to change his sheets this morning? Jill rushed down to his room, pulled off the bedding, and dumped it in the washer.

"Hey, Markie," she said cheerfully as she put new sheets on his bed. "Did you know we're having a party tonight? Or I guess *I'm* having a party, but you're invited if you want to come. I don't know if you'll have a good time, but maybe there'll be someone you like here. And you can meet my friend Vanessa. She really liked your drawings. She's an artist too."

Markie didn't say anything.

"Would you like to meet another artist?" Jill asked him.

"No," said Markie. "And I don't want to have a party."

"Well, we're already having it," said Jill. "It's too late to call it off."

"They better stay in the living room then. They can't come in my room."

"Markie!"

What was the matter with him? Jill decided to leave him alone, to see if he'd get over it. Probably he was still embarrassed about wetting his bed.

"Where's Mommy?" Markie asked her, walking over to look out the window.

"Still at work. She won't get back until late."

"When's Daddy coming home?"

126

Really, Truly, Everything's Fine

"I don't know, Markie!" Jill snapped, her temper fraying. "No one tells me anything either!"

Jill left Markie in his room drawing, then straightened up the house and put away a few breakables. After sniffing the hall to be sure it didn't smell of urine anymore, she took a quick shower and put on clean jeans and her rust-colored sweater because she still had to fix Markie dinner and didn't want to be caught looking a mess.

"Pizza okay, Markie?" she asked him, poking her head into his room.

Markie nodded.

Jill took a pepperoni pizza out of the freezer and slipped it into the oven. Halfway through the baking time, she rearranged the pepperoni into a smiley face to make up to Markie for snapping at him.

As Markie sat down at the table, she looked at her watch—she was so nervous! She didn't even know what time Ric had invited people for.

"Something wrong with the pizza, Markie?" she asked. He hadn't even noticed the smiley face.

"It's okay."

"Are *you* okay? Did something bad happen at school?"

Markie was silent. Jill crouched down next to him. Clearly he was distressed about something. But before she could say anything to him, a car came screaming down the hill and she jumped up, terrified, certain the car was going to come right into the house. Trembling all over, she rushed to the door and saw Vanessa getting out of the car along with Ric and some guy she didn't recognize. The two guys started taking boxes out of the trunk.

Vanessa came to the door. "Who *is* that?" Jill whispered to her.

Vanessa shrugged. "It must be Ric's brother. They look pretty much alike. They picked me up on my way up the hill."

"He's not in middle school, is he, if he's old enough to drive?"

"I guess they needed him to get all the stuff over here. I wonder if he'll stay." Vanessa's eyes were sparkling with excitement. And Jill suddenly noticed something else—Vanessa was wearing makeup!

"Hey, you look really nice," Jill told her.

"This is going to be so cool!" Vanessa turned and peered outside again. "Do you think we should go help them?"

"Yeah, let me get my jacket."

By the time Jill got outside, other kids and a few more cars were coming down the driveway. Ric and his brother were carrying boxes into the kitchen and putting them on the kitchen table, including a case of beer. Someone had already plugged in a CD player and turned on some loud music. Markie had apparently taken his pizza and fled into his bedroom.

"Hey, I don't think—," began Jill, looking at the beer.

"What?" said Ric. "There's a problem?"

"Well, the soft drinks and stuff are fine, and I know you went to a lot of trouble. And I really appreciate it. But the beer—I mean, my mom would have a fit if—like, what if the police—?"

"Oh, come off it, Jill, no one will know! Besides, I'd think your parents would be used to having the cops here."

Jill's heart stopped. She looked around wildly. Micah

and two of his friends had just entered the kitchen, along with a few of the most popular girls in Jill's class—did they think the same thing Ric did? That everyone could have this big illegal bash of a party at her house because her dad was already some kind of criminal?

"I still don't think—," Jill began.

"Forget it, there's no way I'm lugging it back outside," Ric said abruptly and turned to high-five some more people who were just arriving. Jill started to panic. How many people had Ric invited? She'd never seen some of these people, and a lot of them looked as old as Ric's brother. One guy in a camouflage jacket took a flask out of his back pocket and swigged something down. The music was so loud now the floor was rocking.

"Vanessa," Jill hissed, "you've got to help me. Please, this is too crazy. It's going to be a zoo by the time it's finished. How can I get them out of here?"

"I don't think you can. They look to me like they're here to stay. And if you do, every kid in this town's going to be mad at you. But don't worry, people have parties like this all the time. I don't think anything happens except you have a big mess to clean up afterward."

"Look, now Ariel's smoking!" said Jill. "We don't even have any ashtrays! I've got to tell them to leave. How am I going to make everyone hear me?"

"Come on, Jill, chill," Vanessa protested. "Let it go for at least an hour or two. This may be the only party I get to go to all year!"

"I don't care—you're the one who got me into this and you have to get me out of it! I don't care what they think of me! Maybe I should call the police or something."

"Oh, man, I've created a Frankenstein." Vanessa groaned and took a deep breath. "Okay, here's what I'll do," she said. "I'll get Ric and his brother to put out the word that everyone needs to leave and then I'll help them carry their stuff back out to the car. You wait here, and don't do anything stupid."

Jill could have told her Ric wouldn't be any help, but Vanessa was gone before she could stop her. Numbly she watched Vanessa cross the kitchen to where Ric was standing. She said something to him, and he looked Jill's way, then shrugged and turned his back. Vanessa tried Micah, who barely interrupted his conversation with Missy Evans. He had one arm around Missy and the other around Sandy Tsao. *One more lie,* Jill thought angrily. Her eyes stung with tears and she brushed them away impatiently. Vanessa turned back to her and spread her arms out helplessly.

Jill felt the blood rush to her head. How could they just ignore her? Without thinking further, she grabbed a pot and a big slotted spoon from the counter, unplugged the CD player, climbed up on a kitchen chair, and started banging on the pot. The room quieted for a moment.

"Hey, what's with turning off the music?" somebody complained.

"I want you all to leave," Jill said in an even voice that seemed to be coming from someone else. "I'm sorry, but this is a big mistake, and everyone has to go. Please. Right now."

"Tell 'em, Jill!" yelled someone, and then a few people laughed; and moments later everyone was talking and smoking and the music was playing again, as if nothing had happened. A few more kids pushed into the kitchen and grabbed cans of beer; others made their way from the kitchen to the family room with soft drinks in their hands. Vanessa crossed to where Jill was standing by the counter, and the two of them stared through the blue smoke at the crowd. "We're dead," said Vanessa. "We might as well start packing up. Maybe in California they won't have heard of us, but any chance of social life for us here in the Midwest is gone and done for."

A white fury seized Jill. This wasn't about Vanessa, and it wasn't about anyone's social life; it wasn't even about Dad or about Mom's not being here. It was about her, Jill, a person who was sick of liars and people looking through her and twisting her life till it suited their purposes. This was her house, and there were too many stupid people in it, and she hated this party, and she wanted them all to leave. If they thought they could take advantage of her just because her dad had gotten in trouble, well, let them think again! With trembling fingers she grabbed the phone off the hook and dialed 911, which was the only number she could think of, even though she wasn't sure this was a real emergency. The person who answered the phone was calm and businesslike and listened to her with great seriousness; Jill could have wept with relief.

She got up on the chair again and banged on the pot. "I just thought you should know," she yelled above the din. "The police are on their way."

"Everyone fade!" yelled Ric's brother, grabbing the half-full case of beer. There was a sudden scramble as people began looking for their coats and rushing past Jill toward the door. Jill heard cars start up in the driveway and saw headlights flash on, and then suddenly the yellow lights were mixed with flashing blue ones and someone screamed, "Is there a back way?" and Jill just sat down at the kitchen table and put her head in her hands and waited for it to be over.

chapter 24

The police department had sent two officers, a man and a woman. Officer Crandall, the woman, came in to find Jill, asked her a few questions, then told her to stay put until everything was under control. Most of the party guests, as Officer Crandall called them, had evidently left on their own. A few cars were still left in the driveway; Officer Crandall guessed the drivers couldn't get them turned around quickly enough, so they'd abandoned them rather than have to talk to the police.

Jill listened and nodded, but she really didn't care about the details. It was such a relief having someone else dealing with things. Officer Crandall had asked for Jill's mother's phone number, and Jill knew her mom might get into trouble about the beer at the party, but she figured that was Mom's problem. It was all Jill could do to handle her own problems, and she wasn't even sure she could do that anymore. One thing she *was* sure of though: If she found someone to help her through this mess, it wasn't going to be one of her parents or even Keith and Charlotte, who were off celebrating their anniversary just when she needed them; it was going to be someone *helpful*, someone calm and businesslike, like the person who answered her call to the police. Someone who listened and took her seriously and then actually followed up to make things better for her and Markie.

Markie! Jill's heart dropped. Where was he? He must be terrified! She raced down the hall to his room, but he wasn't there. He wasn't anywhere. Jill fought back panic and ran outside to get Officer Crandall. She would know what to do.

"When was the last time you saw him?" Officer Crandall asked her.

"Before the party started." Jill's breath was coming fast, and she was shaking. "He was in the kitchen, eating his pizza. And then when people started coming, he went back to his room. But he's not there! I can't find him anywhere!"

"Little boys seldom just disappear," said Officer Crandall calmly. "Let's go back inside and look again."

But it was as if Markie had taken a page from his Dino-man cartoons and vaporized. Jill watched Officer Crandall's expression harden as they went from room to room.

"Is his coat in the closet?" she asked Jill.

Jill ran to see. "It's not here," she said, barely able to speak. "And I know he put it there when he got home—I saw him."

"I'm going to radio for more help," Officer Crandall told Jill. "At least if the coat's gone, it's a sign he probably left on his own. Just stay right here till I get back to you. Your mom's on her way."

What did the policewoman mean, Markie had probably left on his own? Jill's throat went dry with fear. Had Officer Crandall really been thinking there was a chance someone had *taken* him? Jill remembered suddenly how worried Mom had been the night of the hobby show that one of the people Dad had been hanging out with might have gotten back at him by hurting her or Markie. No, that couldn't be! Jill started shouting her brother's name, pleading with him to answer her. She checked all the rooms again, and the closets, and under the beds. All she found was dust and Markie's long-lost Pooh bear, which she pressed to her cheek and then laid carefully on Markie's bed.

Mom arrived before Officer Crandall came back inside. Her face was gray as she walked through the door.

"I don't know what happened, Mom," Jill told her desperately, her eyes filling with tears. "I was here in the kitchen the whole time the party was going on. I'd have seen him if he came past me. I thought he was in his room."

Mom looked as if she were having trouble processing what Jill was telling her. "They think he must have gone out the front." Her voice was hollow. Then she looked around wildly. "Why is everyone just standing out there? Why aren't they out finding him?" She wheeled about. "Jill, put your coat on. We're going to look for him. I'm not waiting here—anything could have happened to him by now! I don't care what—"

Officer Crandall came back into the room. "It's best if you stay right here, Mrs. Rider," she said gently. "Why don't you come sit down at the table? When Markie gets back, the first thing he's going to want to do is see his mom. And believe me, we're already doing everything we can to find him."

Officer Crandall took Mom's arm and guided her to a chair. Mom pulled Jill down next to her, gripping Jill's hand so tightly it hurt.

"We checked with Mr. Rider—I think he may be coming out to help with the search," Officer Crandall told Mom in her calm, efficient voice.

Mom started shaking her head.

"Apparently your husband's been with his lawyer all evening. But until we can talk more to him, we need you to think—is there a particular place Markie might have gone if he was upset? Some place he likes to hide? Someone he might confide in?"

"I don't know, he's never done anything like this before, he could be anywhere! Please just go look for him, just find him—I promise you I'll wait here, but someone needs to be out looking for him—he'll freeze out there! And there are cars up and down that road, and he's never been out after dark on his own—"

"Did anyone ask the Carrolls?" Jill put in quickly. "I know they were going out, but Markie might have waited till they got back."

"They got home a few minutes ago," said Officer Crandall. "They haven't seen Markie, but Mr. Carroll's coming over in a few minutes to get briefed. The temperature's dropping fast, and we're trying to get as many people out there as possible to help the police."

Abruptly Mom moved to rise, then sank back in her chair, eyes fixed on the back door. Jill patted her awkwardly, feeling Mom's shoulder quiver under her hand, then tense up sharply when Keith's face appeared in the glass panel. Keith entered the kitchen in a blast of cold air and suggested that Jill come out searching with him—Jill knew Markie better than anyone and might be able to spot places he'd hole up in or things he might have dropped along the way. Officer Crandall agreed; and finally Mom gave permission, but only if Keith promised not to let Jill out of his sight.

"Try to be hopeful," Keith told Mom as Jill came back into the kitchen with her coat. "If I know Markie, he hasn't gone very far."

"Just find him for me," Mom said in a whisper. "Please, Keith?"

"That's my plan," said Keith. He buttoned up his red plaid lumber jacket. "Ready, Jill?" he said. "Let's get out there and look."

It was so dark outside! The police in the driveway had turned off their flashing lights (so as not to frighten Markie if he decided to return on his own, Keith told Jill), and the woods in back of the house loomed thick and black. With Keith close beside her, Jill picked her way among the leafless trees, willing herself to concentrate, to think as Markie might have done. Where might he be hiding? The flashlights she and Keith held sent long fingers of yellow light ahead of them, but the darkness was disorienting, and the ground, part ice and part slippery mud, was treacherous. Twice Jill's foot slid out in front of her, and she would have fallen had it not been for Keith's hand at her elbow. Markie, she thought, *where are you? Where could you have gone?* Being in the woods didn't feel right; Markie was afraid of the dark, and he hated being cold.

Off in the distance Jill heard the muffled voices of other searchers and saw an occasional strobe of light. Anyone with information was supposed to start a chain of calls to pass it on to the search party. Jill huddled down in her pea coat. "Are you sure your cell phone's on?" she whispered to Keith, though she knew the phone must be working.

Keith pulled the phone from his pocket.

"I've got the ringer turned up as loud as it can go."

Of course he did. Jill was grateful he hadn't made a fuss about her asking. She was also grateful he didn't insist on chatting with her. She didn't think she could bear conversation right now. She could feel her brain activity reducing itself to one single track, the track that would locate her brother. That was all she wanted. If Markie was found, she didn't care about anything else.

Through the tangled black tree branches, Jill suddenly saw yellow lights, stationary ones. There were three houses on Murray Lane whose property backed up against theirs and the Carrolls' with the woods in between. "Let's go all the way through to Murray Lane," she told Keith, her teeth chattering from the damp and cold. She jammed her hands farther down in her pockets. "Maybe Markie found a garage to hide in or something. I don't think he'd have stayed in the woods."

Keith didn't argue; he followed Jill steadily through the trees. A dog barked as they approached the first backyard, and then more flashing blue lights appeared in front of the house—apparently the police were already canvassing these streets. Jill willed Keith's cell phone to ring with news, but it stayed silent.

"Markie," Jill called out. "Markie . . ."

"Keep calling," Keith said. "If he hears you, he's more likely to come out. You're the one he trusts the most right now."

But I was the one who let him leave the house. I never even thought about checking on him.

"Markie, it's Jill," she called, her voice breaking. "The party's over—everyone went home. Please, Markie, we need you to come out now. We just want to take you home."

Please, Markie, be here. If you're here and we find you, I'll be the best sister in the world; I'll do anything you want me to. Please, God, let me find him.

Keith sent his light searching carefully into the four corners of the first yard, behind the garage, in a small area next to a large woodpile. He tried the garage door, but it was locked. Jill knocked on one of the cloudy windows and called Markie's name just in case. No answer.

The dog was barking frantically by now. It probably thought they were robbers. Jill was surprised the people in the house hadn't called the police. But the police were already there.

She shook her head, not sure she was making sense anymore. She was so cold. So frightened.

"Let's try next door," said Keith. "Their garage is open."

This garage was new and very neat, with ladders hanging on the walls and tools arranged neatly in specially built cubbies. There weren't many places to hide.

"Markie?" Jill called softly as Keith swung his light around. "He's not here," she said, turning to Keith. Keith's face looked drawn, and his nose was red.

He shook his head. "Let's call Charlotte and see if

maybe she's heard something," he suggested. "She wanted me to call in from time to time anyway and let her know we were okay."

He pulled the phone from his pocket, and at that moment it rang, a sharp, warbling sound that shattered the night. Jill jumped. She stared at the phone, her heart racing. Quickly Keith put it to his ear.

"Yes? Where? Thank God!" Keith gave Jill a quick thumbs-up sign. "They found him!" he said. "Everything's fine." Then, back to the phone: "Okay, we'll be right there. Does my wife know? No, there are some police cars here, and we can hitch a ride with them. See you in a few."

He switched off the phone, then turned to Jill. "They did it, Jilly! He's okay! He's home! Oh, my heavens, look at you. Are you all right?" Jill was trembling all over, her knees like Jell-O; but Keith quickly swooped down to hold her up. He wasn't as tall as Dad, and he was leaner, but his strong arms around her were so much like Dad's that Jill was overcome by a heart-crushing sense of anguish.

"It's okay, it's going to be all right," Keith soothed her. "Markie's fine, I promise you."

She wanted to tell him it wasn't about Markie, but when she tried to speak, a shuddering sob filled her throat. Helplessly she hid her face in the damp wool of Keith's jacket and burst into tears.

chapter

25

Saturday, April 15

Boy, so much has happened since I last wrote that I
don't know where to start. I was such a mess after the party.
I couldn't stop crying. I never want to go through anything
like that again. It was just about the worst night of my life,
but at least some good things came out of it. The best thing
maybe is Gayla, my social worker. I got her because of the
police. They really pushed Mom after the party to get some
help for me and Markie, and I think she might have been
scared she'd get in trouble if she didn't do what they said.
Mom still doesn't want me to tell Grandma Rider or anyone
we know that we're seeing someone, but I think that's dumb.
Why does it have to be such a big secret?

Anyway, New Milford Police Department to the
rescue! Gayla's great. She said it was really brave and smart
of me the night of the party to call the police when I felt
things were getting out of hand, and that's what I have to
remember most, to ask for help when I need it. And she
made me see that the way things were, everyone was expect-

ing me to be the adult, and I just wasn't ready for it, but why should I be, because I'm not an adult. I still feel awful about that night though, mostly about Markie. I was right— he didn't go to the woods. What he did was sneak out the front, past all the kids in the driveway, and then he walked four houses down the road looking for something to steal! Honestly! He said he wanted to steal something because he thought the police would arrest him, and then he'd get to see Daddy! He wound up taking some garden tools from the Pryors' garage, and then he got scared the police really <u>would</u> take him to jail so he hid at the Loehmans', which is where they found him.

I was worried it was my fault that he did it, because I was the one who told him Daddy had actually stolen stuff, but Gayla said he was probably all mixed up from <u>everything</u> that had gone on, that the truth was what he really needed. I still feel guilty though. But at least Markie has his own social worker now (his is a man), and Markie and Mom sometimes see this guy together, and I'm just so relieved someone's trying to help him.

A couple of people got in big trouble because of the party (Ric's brother included), so now there's a bunch of kids at school who hate me. Micah's friends look at me like I'm this pitiful scum or something, and Micah doesn't look at me at all. But there isn't much I can do about that. Vanessa actually tried to tell them she was the one who called the police because she felt like she was the one who made me have the party and she owed it to me to take the blame. But I don't think anyone believed her. She also told me she tried to stick around the night of the party after the police came so I'd at least have someone I knew with me (Officer Crandall said she kept going around saying, "It's all my fault, it's all my fault"), but the police made her go home (they actually drove her home in a police car!). That night is such a blur to me—when I think about it, all I see in my head are those flashing blue lights and lots of people all over our house and yard. And Markie huddled in a corner with fourteen blankets wrapped around him and Mom practically hysterical when Keith and I got home.

The only thing good at school is the can-sculpture show. Vanessa's been helping with that, and Mary Kate and some other kids are helping too, and while Vanessa and M.K. probably aren't ever going to be friends, at least they're not trashing each other all the time. It's like Vanessa is really creative and Mary Kate is really practical and I'm somewhere in the middle. But Mrs. Eisenstadt thinks we're doing great and the show's going to be a big success. And do you know what Russell's sculpture is going to be? A can made out of cans! The funny thing is, it's pretty good!

Gayla says this diary is a good place to write about my feelings, but it's really hard to write about Dad now, even though I can write about almost everything else. Gayla said something interesting though. She never, like, says anybody's bad or good; she just lets me make up my own mind about things. But when we were talking about Daddy the other day, she said she thought one of the things that made me so strong was all the loving I got from him when I was little. I'm still mad at him though, and at Mom too, though not her so much anymore because I think she was feeling as awful as we were and she didn't know what to do either. And I guess she was getting panicked about money and that was why she spent so much time working. Anyway, she's trying now, but it's still really sad in the house, and I don't know when that's ever going to be over. Mary Kate doesn't know how lucky she is to have Charlotte and Keith for her parents. I wish they were mine, not hers, but they're not—they're hers. At least I have Gayla, who's all mine for the time being.

Linda Leopold Strauss

If you're wondering why I started writing again today, it's probably because I'm going to go see Dad tomorrow. I'm going to take the bus by myself to his apartment. Mom didn't want me to go on my own, but Vanessa told me what bus line to take, and I don't want Mom looking over my shoulder. It's been ages since I've seen Dad, and I'm not even sure what I'm going to say. I hope it goes all right. It's pretty awful to see articles about your dad in the paper that call him a con man and a liar. And to know your father is going to jail for 13 months. He's only got a few more days left to get his stuff together. But he promised me he'd be there tomorrow so I could tell him good-bye.

chapter

26

Jill stood outside her dad's apartment door and hesitated a moment before pressing the bell. Dad knew she was here—he'd buzzed her upstairs—but she could still leave; the elevator went down as well as up. Dad would probably think she was crazy if she left, but lots of people thought she was crazy these days. At least Gayla wasn't one of them. Jill would be forever grateful to her for that.

Nervously Jill tucked her hair back behind her ear. *Do it*, she told herself. *Now. Get it over with.*

Quickly she put out a finger and rang the bell.

Almost immediately the door opened, and Dad stood before her. He looked just as she remembered him—every hair in place, khaki pants, navy golf shirt. If she hadn't known what was going on, she'd have sworn he was headed for the Club. Maybe he was.

Maybe he'd just postponed teeing off till he had this
little visit with her.

Keep it together, Jill.

"Jilly!" said Dad. "You found me all right? You didn't
have any trouble?"

Jill shook her head.

"Come on in. How are you? How's Markie?"

"We're fi—" Jill caught herself. "We're okay," she
said.

She looked around. Dad had fixed up the apartment nicely, had even bought plants and hung pictures
on the walls. He didn't look in the least as if he'd started packing—wasn't he supposed to be going to jail in a
couple of days? Did you have to pack a suitcase for jail?
There were so many questions to ask, so many questions she was afraid to ask. But she didn't have to get
everything settled today, Gayla had told her. Just see
how you feel; put one toe in at a time.

"How are *you?*" Jill asked her father. He hadn't
hugged her yet; that was different. Maybe he was
afraid to. Maybe he didn't know what her reaction
would be.

"I'm fine. It's good to see you." He put a finger to
her cheek, and she caught a whiff of familiar after-
shave. "Come sit. Are you going to stay for lunch?"

Jill shook her head. The thought of lunch actually
made her feel nauseated. Did Dad really think this was
a normal visit? "I just came to say good-bye," she told
him. "Are you going to stop at the house and see
Markie before you go?"

"I'm certainly going to try. I was just talking with
your mom about what was best. I've missed you guys."

Jill knew she was supposed to say she'd missed Dad too. Actually she missed him more now, right here, than she had for ages. The distance between them made her ache physically. Would it always be like this from now on?

"I know you're upset with me, Jill," Dad pleaded. "But won't you at least try to forgive me? I can't stand having to leave with you hating me—"

"I never said I hated you. It's just that—"

"I know what I did was really hurtful. But if you think about it, maybe by testifying I wound up doing some good too. So actually—"

Jill stared at him. "Don't try to make me think what you did was good—I can't believe you're saying that. It was awful! It was the worst thing that ever happened to me!"

"Ah, Jill, I never meant—"

"I don't care what you meant; it's what you did!" Jill told him hotly. "I wish I hadn't even come here to say good-bye to you!"

"I'm glad you did," Dad said. "I'm not sure when we'll see each other again."

And whose fault is that? Jill wanted to scream at him. Gayla had said she could visit Dad when he was in jail, but Jill wasn't at all sure she could bear that.

"Will you at least write to me?" Dad asked.

"I don't know," said Jill, fighting hard to keep her voice under control. "You write me first. Only don't expect me to write back that everything's fine and great and we can't wait until you come home. I'm not going to write anything that's not true! And you'd better tell me the truth from now on too, or else I don't want to hear from you. Not one single letter!"

"But—"

"I mean it, Dad! You got my head so messed up, I don't even know where it is some days! I think it's horrible that you did that! So if you're going to do stuff like that again, you can just go find someone else to write to!"

Jill could hardly believe she'd said all those things to her father. She'd put her toe in the water all right; she'd rushed in practically up to her eyebrows. She wondered if Gayla had been right after all, if back in those good years she'd had with her dad, he had given her the strength to stand up even against him. Life could be amazingly complicated. Maybe someday she'd understand it all better. But she was learning.

Jill thought back suddenly to when Mary Kate thought Vanessa told fortunes with tarot cards. She wondered what it would be like to know her future, then decided she didn't really want to know ahead of time. One thing was for sure though—she was only going to let people blame her for things she'd done, not things someone else in her family did. She was going to be just "Jill-who's-Jill," and anyone who wanted to be her friend would have to know that about her.

Her father clearly had some things to learn too. But she'd done her part by coming to say good-bye, and now it was time to go home.

"I need to leave now," she told her father. He nodded, looking suddenly sad and old. Despite herself, Jill felt like crying.

"I love you, Jilly," he said, walking across the apartment with her.

Really, Truly, Everything's Fine

She checked the statement for truth. But she knew it was true. It was something she could take with her.

"I love you too," she whispered, so softly she wasn't sure he could hear it. Then quickly she turned and walked out the door.